W9-CVY-121

★

Tony pulled open one of the big doors to Mystic Hall. The lights were off but for a beam of red light aiming at the stage. Janvilhelm sat at the piano.

Rather, the grand piano pretty much sat on him. The upper half of Janvilhelm's body had been all but swallowed by the cover of the piano.

Tony approached slowly. "Janvilhelm?" he whispered, in trembling tones. Was it the cold of Sedona or the apparent coldness of his friend, Janvilhelm? Tony touched Janvilhelm's sleeve. "John?"

Still no answer.

Shaking, Tony raised the heavy lid of the piano. It took some effort. He hissed when he saw the splash of blood that engulfed Janvilhelm's skull and spattered the inside of the piano itself.

★

"Wacky characters, liquid prose, frequent humor, and a decidedly light plot place this in the fun, breeze-to-read category."

—Library Journal

"He (J. R. Ripley) has that touch of the bizarre, the outre, the silly... You'll enjoy this book."

—The Oklahoma Tribune

J.R. Ripley

Skulls of Sedona

WORLDWIDE.

TORONTO • NEW YORK • LONDON
AMSTERDAM • PARIS • SYDNEY • HAMBURG
STOCKHOLM • ATHENS • TOKYO • MILAN
MADRID • WARSAW • BUDAPEST • AUCKLAND

If you purchased this book without a cover you should be aware
that this book is stolen property. It was reported as "unsold and
destroyed" to the publisher, and neither the author nor the
publisher has received any payment for this "stripped book."

SKULLS OF SEDONA

A Worldwide Mystery/July 2001

First published by Beachfront Publishing.

ISBN 0-373-26390-2

Copyright © 2000 by J. R. Ripley.
All rights reserved. No part of this book may be reproduced
or transmitted in any form or by any means, electronic or
mechanical, including photocopying, recording or by any
information storage and retrieval system, without permission
in writing from the publisher. For information, contact:
Beachfront Publishing, P.O. Box 81122, Boca Raton, FL
33481 U.S.A.

Email: Beachpub@aol.com

All characters in this book are fictitious, and any resemblance to
actual persons, living or dead, is purely coincidental.

® and TM are trademarks of Harlequin Enterprises Limited.
Trademarks indicated with ® are registered in the United States
Patent and Trademark Office, the Canadian Trade Marks Office
and in other countries.

Printed in U.S.A.

Somewhere a bear runs free...

ONE

TONY KOZOL edged away from the precipice and stared down the deserted highway. The forty degree chill being served up on a twenty mile an hour gust of wind tore through his flimsy t-shirt and jeans.

Leave it to the airline to lose his suitcase.

It was a good thing he'd carried his guitar aboard the airliner despite the stewardess's protests. Or else they would have lost that too.

Tony recognized the distant rumble of a semi-tractor trailer as it rose up the mountain. He waved and the truck blew past him as if he hadn't existed. Maybe he didn't.

The smell of burnt diesel fuel settled around him like dime-store cologne as Tony glared at the front of his Chevy rental.

The driver's side tire was still flat.

Tony reached through the open window, plucked the key from the ignition and unlocked the trunk. He found a spare tire and a jack. The jack looked impossible to use, especially considering the precarious slope upon which the car was perched.

How far was Sedona? Who knew...?

Arizona was as alien to him as the moon. And up here in the high desert, forty-five hundred feet above sea level, it was just about as cold. Gone less than a day, Kozol was already missing the warmth of south Florida. Who knew sea level could be so enchanting?

Interstate 17 may as well have been the road to a ghost town. Where were all the cars?, he wondered. I-17 was the main road from Phoenix to Sedona, so Kozol had been told. All the way to Flagstaff. Maybe it was National Don't Go to Flagstaff Day.

Tony blew warm air onto his fingers and picked up the icy lug wrench. He hated working on cars. Tony squatted, popped the hubcap and diligently attacked the first lug nut. It wouldn't budge.

"Great."

Tony heard the crunch of tires on gravel and turned. A red Jeep Wrangler, caked with a generous layer of mud, had pulled up behind his car. It bore a California license plate. A tall redheaded woman leapt from within. Cute. Tony watched her with eyes the color of an autumn oak leaf.

Kozol was suddenly aware of his own personal shortcomings. He stood just under six foot. His brown, already naturally wavy hair had that tousled look that only a night sleeping on a jet or an hour in a wind tunnel could capture. He'd gone without a shower and was unshaven. He was hungry. But then he could probably stand to lose a couple of pounds. Though he preferred to think of it as muscle toning.

There was nothing so striking about Tony Kozol as the surroundings in which he found himself.

Tony waited for her to speak.

"In these parts," she said, assessing the situation, "if that was a horse, they'd shoot it."

"Got a gun I can borrow?"

"Sorry, left my six-shooter back at the ranch," said the redhead. "Anything I can do?"

"No," said Tony. "There's a bolt driven through the front tire and I can't even get the lugs off. So the spare's useless."

"Are you a member of an auto club?"

"It's a rental." Tony rose and rubbed his frozen fingers. His savior appeared to be about his age, maybe younger, in her late twenties or early thirties, he suspected, with light red hair and emerald green eyes.

"Better still," said the girl. "Leave it here. Let them deal with it."

"Is that an offer of a ride?"

"Sure. At least as far as Sedona. That's where I'm stopping."

"Me too," said Tony. "Thanks." He held out his hand. "I'm Tony. Tony Kozol."

"Virginia Garner." She looked at Tony's vehicle. "Have you got anything in there that you need?"

"Just a sec—" Tony tossed the lug wrench, spare and jack in the trunk and slammed it shut. The sharp sound echoed down the canyon. He rolled up the driver's side window, grabbed his guitar case from the backseat, stuck the car key under the front seat and pushed the lock down on the door before closing it.

"That's it? Not even a jacket?"

"I only flew in this morning to Phoenix," explained Tony. "The airline lost my suitcase. They said they would call when they find it."

"Good luck," Virginia said. "Better toss the guitar in back and let's get going. It looks like we might be in for a rare rain storm."

Tony glanced upward. The sky was gray and the clouds scuttled quickly across the wide sky.

Virginia climbed into the Jeep. That was when Tony noticed that there were no doors. He tossed his guitar into the open back and sat.

"There's an old blanket on the floor back there, if you want it."

"Nah, I'll be alright," said Tony.

"Suit yourself," replied Virginia. She gunned

the gas pedal and the Jeep shot away. Wind whipped unrelentingly through the passenger cabin.

Before long Tony swallowed his male ego and silently reached back and found an old navy blue wool blanket. It smelled of gasoline and dog. He wrapped himself up and shut his eyes. It wasn't so much that he was tired as it was the way the girl drove. Like a maniac.

A maniac with no doors.

"WAKE UP, TONY," Virginia nudged Kozol with her elbow. One hand held the wheel. "This is it, beautiful downtown Sedona." She pulled the Jeep off to the side and parked along a row of art galleries, bookstores and gift shops. A mirror image occupied the opposite side of the street.

Tony groaned. Every muscle ached. His nose was cold as an icicle. "Thanks. You don't know how to get to someplace called—" Tony searched through his pockets and retrieved a brochure, "Red Rock Resort by any chance, do you?"

Virginia's face turned quizzical. "Is that where you're staying?"

"Yes, for a couple of nights."

Virginia laughed. "Me too. Damn, and I passed it back before the fork in the road coming into town. Oh well." She made a broad u-turn and headed back down the road. "Are you here for the Crystal Magic of the Skulls Conference?"

"Sort of," said Tony. Inwardly, he groaned. Crystal Magic of the Skulls. Numbskulls was more like it.

"It's fascinating, isn't it?" said the redhead, as she drove slowly past a rider on horseback. "Did you know that Maggie and Azul are supposed to be thousands of years old?"

"Who?"

"Maggie and Azul. Magdelena and Azultican. The crystal skulls, you know?"

Tony shook his head no.

"You don't know much about this stuff, do you?"

"I'm afraid not."

"Then why are you here?"

"Long story," Tony replied.

"Okay," said Virginia. "Well anyway, Maggie and Azul are supposed to contain the wisdom of an ancient race from a distant star. According to the history, an alien race left the skulls here on earth for we humans to find and eventually to discover the information that is stored inside them."

Tony made appropriate noises to feign interest.

"There is even a mention of them in early Olmec legend."

"And who are the Olmecs? More aliens?"

Virginia grinned. Her red hair spun in the mountain air like streaks of sunlight the color of the surrounding red rocks. "The Olmec peoples inhabited the Veracruz region of what is now central Mexico thousands of years ago. Haven't you ever seen pictures of those large, helmeted monoliths they created?"

"Maybe. Look there's the sign for the Red Rock Resort. There, on the right." If he could just get checked into his room and call the rental agency and the airline...

Virginia nodded and parked at the main entrance. The Red Rock Resort occupied a good twenty acres or so of prime Sedona hills along the edge of Oak Creek with vistas of the magnificent, surrounding red rock country, including nearby Elephant Rock. The resort's architecture was reminiscent of Native American adobe styling with relatively minor modern touches visible to the eye. The high flat mesa, upon which was built the Sedona Airport, was to the west.

Tony grabbed his guitar from the back and opened the door for Virginia.

A young girl raised her head from behind a long, western styled wood counter, whose face bore the carved figures of cacti, cowboy boots and saddles. She smiled. "May I help you?"

"I'm checking in," Virginia said.

"Two?"

"No, we're not together," explained Virginia.

"Oh, I see. Name?"

Virginia filled out her registration form while Tony waited, his guitar at his heels.

"Hello."

Tony turned. A stunning woman with shiny black hair and bright blue eyes greeted him with a smile that seemed both cool and warm at once. "Hi," stuttered Tony.

"I'm Suzette." She held out her hand and Tony took it. "Are you with Janvilwelm?"

"Yes," said Tony.

"You must be Tony Kozol. I've been expecting you."

"That's right. Are you with the conference?"

"Yes, I am associated with the event."

Virginia turned and eyed the light skinned woman cooly. "Miss Aristotle is displaying the magic crystal skulls."

"That's right," said Suzette with an unrevealing smile. "And you are?"

"Virginia Garner."

"Pleased to meet you. I hope you will enjoy the conference."

"Believe me," Virginia replied, "I intend to. If there's anything you need, Tony, let me know.

I've got a couple of spare flannel shirts I could loan you.''

"Is there a problem, Tony?" inquired Miss Aristotle.

"Oh, it's nothing. The airline has misplaced my luggage."

"Tsk, tsk." She shook her head. "Let's see what we can do about that." Suzette took Tony by the arm and led him away. "See you at the reception tonight, Miss Garner."

"Fine, I could use a good, long bubble bath anyway."

"Yes, I'm sure you could," replied Suzette, with a smile and a quick turn of the heel.

Virginia was left standing there, a half-scowl across her face.

"But what about my registration?"

"Just a formality," said Suzette. "It can be handled later."

"And my guitar—" Tony had left it sitting on the hard Mexican tile floor. He didn't want to lose that too. It was practically all he had left.

Suzette waved to a porter who stood near the Help Desk. "Please take care of that for Mr. Kozol, won't you?"

The porter nodded and hustled over to take charge of Tony's guitar.

"Let me show you around." Suzette led Tony

past reception, to the right, down a sparsely furnished hallway and into a conference room. The bronze placard on the wall at the side of the door gave its name as Mystic Hall. "This is where our ceremony will take place this evening."

Tony looked about. "I see." The conference room was no more than fifty or sixty feet on each side. It would have been a square, but one wall was crooked. Was this intentional or had the architect and building crew been spaced out on peyote? Kozol figured either was just as plausible. There were dozens of rows of padded chairs stretched across the room with a small stage rising at the far end. A podium and empty table occupied the center of the stage.

"I understand that you are also an attorney, Mr. Kozol? How unusual."

"Was an attorney. I—gave it up."

"Mmmm," she said, a slight pout on her electric, near purple, lips. "I'm sure you find being a musician far more rewarding."

"Something like that. And call me Tony, please."

"Yes, Tony." Miss Aristotle turned a step closer. "I thought perhaps you might be able to answer a legal question for me. A small one, really."

Kozol shrugged. "I'll try."

"It's about contracts—"

"That wasn't exactly my specialty but what's the question?"

"Well, supposing one has a contract for services with another person or a company," she began, "but it was not written by a lawyer exactly. Are the terms binding?"

Tony considered. "I suppose they could be. You don't have to be a lawyer or hire one to write a contract. If it was written properly and signed and witnessed…"

"Oh, I'm sure it was."

"There's not some problem here is there? With the conference organizers?" Kozol had visions of his paycheck flying out the window like a UFO, never to be seen again.

"Oh, no. It's nothing like that. Nothing at all. You see, I do many events such as these and sometimes contracts are required. And, silly me, I'll sign just about anything. Sometimes I wonder what I'm getting myself into."

She smiled and Tony felt his knees buckling.

"Well, I'd be more careful if I were you."

Suzette agreed, then abruptly changed the subject. "Maggie and Azul will be located there," she explained, "on stage. Along with Janvilhelm and yourself, of course."

"The skulls are going to be on stage with us

tonight? I thought the concert was tomorrow evening?'' Tony felt a wave of panic wash up and down his body, from his cold toes to his spine. He and John hadn't even rehearsed once!

"This is merely the opening ceremony. Chief Howling Wind will perform a blessing on us. This is sacred ground, you know."

"No, I didn't know."

"The entire Sedona-Oak Creek area is alive with multiple vortices."

"I'm afraid I don't follow you, Miss Aristotle." Kozol was beginning to wonder if this whole trip was worth the money his old friend, John Ryan, was paying him for the gig. A weekend of playing backup guitar was what he had expected. Not the prattle of a nest of New Age spiritualists.

"A vortex is an energy field located on the surface of the earth. As I started to say, this region of the Coconino National Forest which we are in is a proven center of such vortices. Even the early Native American inhabitants of the region were aware of this. They called it sacred ground. We call it a vortex. Those who are sensitive can feel it within."

"I'm afraid I don't feel a thing."

Suzette laughed. "Perhaps it's only too soon. I sense an aura of spirit about you. Those who are sensitive to a vortex can absorb its power. Some vortexes are magnetic, others electrical. They can have an energizing or a calming effect. It all depends on the person, their sensitivity to a particular vortex and their place in the universe at that moment.''

''Like a tingling in the toes?'' joked Kozol.

Suzette replied, ''Like a tingling in the mind. Do you believe in God, Tony?''

''Sort of.''

''The Native Americans believe that everything on earth is alive and possesses spirit.''

Tony thought about that. ''I suppose that makes sense.''

''Not only people or even animals. The hills, the trees, the rocks, the rivers and streams—''

''My guitar?''

''Exactly!'' said Suzette. ''Your guitar and Janvilwelm Rein Wunderkind's keyboards will also channel this spirit tonight. The crystal mystic skulls, Maggie and Azul, will, if we are blessed, also impart their wisdom and spirit upon you and Janvilhelm and upon us all, here tonight.''

Tony rubbed his unshaven chin. Suddenly he felt like either shaving his stubble or cutting his throat. And the girl was so pretty too. Pity. He'd met two attractive women in one short day. One was a lunatic. The other was a space cadet.

Some things never change.

TWO

TONY TOSSED his guitar onto the spare bed and himself onto the other. Kozol was too tired to even undress. It was all he could do to kick off his sneakers.

Where was John?

According to Suzette, he and John were giving some type of performance that evening, only hours away. Tony closed his eyes and tried to relax. The red light on the bedside telephone was blinking rudely. Ignore it, thought Kozol.

The door opened.

"I'm sorry, I thought this was my room—" A small, slightly overweight woman in her mid to late thirties, with cocoa brown hair cut short around her face stood in the doorway. Her nose was diminutive and sharp. Her eyes were dark. A scent of gardenias seemed to accompany her.

Tony sat up on the edge of the bed. "I don't think so. Room 405?"

The woman looked confused. She held a crumpled brown paper sack in her left hand. A cloth purse hung from her shoulder. "Uh, no. I mean, I'm not sure. I'd better check with the desk."

She clutched her purse across her chest and left in a hurry.

"Wait!" began Tony. "How did you get in—" the door slammed shut, "here."

Kozol jumped off the bed and opened the door. He looked up and down the walkway. The woman was gone. "Damn."

Tony turned. The room's door had closed behind him. He twisted the handle. It had locked automatically. So how had the woman gotten in? Did the hotel give her a duplicate key? It was possible. The keys were the new magnetic plastic card variety. A human versus computer foul-up was always a possibility in this brave new world.

Tony reached in his pocket for his own card. "Damn it, again!" Peering through the open curtains his own room card was clearly visible on the little round table beside the window.

Barefoot but for thin cotton socks, Tony headed along the freezing pavement and made his way across the parking lot. Kozol headed in a diagonal in the direction he hoped led to the main building.

He spotted a housekeeping trolley outside a room on his right and jogged over. Tony stuck his head in the open door. A young maid was cleaning the bathroom mirror. "Excuse me."

She turned. "Yes?"

"I seem to have locked myself out of my room. Do you think you could help me?"

"What room are you in, sir?"

Tony gave his room number.

"I'm sorry. I only do up this section of the hotel. My key won't work in your building. Sorry. Try the front desk."

"I will," said Tony. "Tell me, am I heading in the proper direction?"

"Keep following those steps up, then it's to your right at the top of the stairs."

Tony thanked her and left. He came to a courtyard where a swimming pool gave off a warm mist. Across the pool was what appeared to be a game room and exercise area. Through the glass doors, Kozol spotted Virginia in a slinky pale orange leotard working out inside. She saw him, stopped mid-sit-up and waved. Tony waved back.

Virginia opened the door and called out, "What are you up to? You look like you're freezing!"

"I am," confessed Tony. "I've locked myself out of my room." He wiggled his quickly solidifying toes. "In my stocking feet no less."

Virginia laughed. "You're off to some start this weekend, aren't you?"

Tony could only nod.

"Look, are you going to attend the dinner tonight?"

"I don't know, I suppose so."

"Good. I'll see you there. Eight o'clock, okay?"

"Okay," agreed Tony.

"Now get going before you turn into an ice sculpture."

Tony nodded again and huffed painfully up the remaining steps to the lobby. His lungs stung with every breath. Kozol felt hypothermic and had visions of frostbite and toes and other more relevant body parts being hastily chopped off by surgeons who were paid on a per piece basis.

There was a fireplace in one corner with a sitting area around it. Tony planted himself in front of the blissfully warm flames and absorbed the heat. A couple seated at a red velvet couch, speaking with decidedly British accents, scowled at him. But courtesy be damned, he was cold!

"May I help you, sir?" said a fellow in hotel garb, brown trousers and a white shirt with the Red Rock Resort logo, whom Tony hadn't seen before. The tag pinned to his shirt identified him as Mark Taggert, Assistant Manager. He seemed to look at Kozol askance.

"I-I locked myself out of my room. 405." Kozol shivered involuntarily.

"I see. Your name?"

"Tony Kozol."

"Any I.D., sir?"

Tony shook his head no. "It's in my room."

Mark gave Tony what appeared to be another of his trademark-worthy cynical looks. "Alright Mr. Kozol. I'm Mark, the assistant manager. Let me see what I can do." He scooted behind the counter and punched away at the computer. "Where are you visiting us from, Mr. Kozol?"

"Florida, Ocean Palm." Tony nudged up closer to the fire and raised his feet one by one towards the flames. At this point, he wouldn't have minded if his socks caught fire.

Mark nodded and appeared satisfied. He produced another room key card and set it on the counter. "Here you are. I've made a duplicate. Maybe you should keep one on your person each time you leave your room?"

Tony resisted the urge to reply to the smart ass. Mostly because he couldn't think up a good enough reply. Maybe it was the cold.

"Would you need a ride to your room?" asked Mark solicitously. Maybe he was only anxious to get the unshoed guest from his elegant lobby.

"That would be great," replied Tony, with visions of a comfy warm car with heater at full thrust.

Mark smiled, waved to a porter and softly gave instructions. "Please see Mr. Kozol back to his room."

"Yes, sir," replied the porter. "This way Mr. Kozol, sir."

Tony reluctantly left his spot beside the fire and followed the porter out the front doors. The sun was quickly setting. Darkness was falling like a heavy Hopi rug descending from the sky.

"Hop in." The porter grabbed the wheel. "What's your room number?"

Tony sourly took a seat beside the porter. It was a golf cart. "405," he said with a shiver and a sigh.

The golf cart lurched to a stop at the parking curb outside his room. Tony jumped off. "Thanks." The porter silently drove off. Tony gingerly stepped over the gravel between the parking lot and the sidewalk. The curtain of the room next door seemed to open a crack and then quickly closed again.

Inside his own room, Tony cranked up the heat to maximum, turned the shower on to medium boil, took off all his clothes and jumped in. And he could have stayed there forever if he hadn't opened his eyes and seen the bloated, dead black rat floating on its fat, wet belly, one beady eye staring horribly, emptily up at him.

Kozol let out something between a grunt and a scream. A scrunt. His feet slid as he backpedaled away from the drain, where the rat had been hopelessly drawn. The water was up to Tony's ankles. Dead rat water. Tony scrambled out of the tub and rinsed his feet in the sink, before toweling them dry.

Only then did he reach in and shut off the water that had been left running in the shower/tub. Kozol glanced out of the corner of his eye. The black rat was still there, rolling in the gently draining tub. If only the vermin would fit down the drain!

And was it his overactive imagination or did the bathroom suddenly smell piquantly of boiled rat? Kozol fought his impulse to vomit.

Tony held his breath, wrapped a towel around his waist to protect himself from the ever present chill, and grabbed the telephone. He scanned the face of the phone and punched the number of housekeeping. He got the front desk instead.

"Mark here, can I be of assistance?"

Tony pulled his hair. Of course, it had to be Mark. "This is Mr. Kozol in room 405—"

"Have we lost our key again, sir?"

''No, we have not lost our key,'' Tony replied. ''We have found a rat in our bathtub!''

There was a long silence.

''We don't have rats, sir.''

''There is an ugly black rat floating in my shower,'' said Tony. ''Please have someone come and remove it!''

''Perhaps you've dropped something? A sock, perhaps? As I recall you were wearing black socks when you visited us in the lobby ''

''I wasn't visiting you in the lobby. I'd been locked out of my room. And, by the way, some woman had come into my room earlier while I was lying down. How do you explain that?''

''A woman? In your room, sir?'' said Mark. ''Yes, I can see how that would be a mistake.''

''Very funny. Just send someone in to remove this carcass before I report the incident to the local health department.''

''I'm sure there is no reason for that, Mr. Kozol,'' Mark said soothingly. ''I can see that, perhaps, a tiny deer mouse might have crept into your room while the door was open.''

''The beast's as big as my fist!''

Mark clicked his tongue solicitously. ''I shall send O'Brien. He is in charge of maintenance.''

''That will be fine.'' Tony began to remove the receiver from his ear.

"Perhaps you would like your message now, sir? While I have you on the line."

"Message?" Kozol had forgotten all about the blinking red message light on his telephone.

"Yes, sir. There's a flag on the monitor here indicating that you have had a call to your room. Shall I get it for you?"

"Yes, please do, Mark," said Tony, with what he hoped was unconcealed mockery.

"One moment, while I pull the message file."

Tony heard some clattering, then Mark came back on the phone. "Well?"

Mark cleared his throat. "It says, sir, 'You're a rat'." Mark waited for a response. None was forthcoming. "Sir?"

Tony turned his head toward the bath. The sound of water gurgling down the drain echoed from the tub, and then silence. A rat. A dead rat, thought Kozol, uneasily. "Does the message say who it is from?"

"No, sir. Would you like a copy? I can make a printout if you like."

Tony said, "That won't be necessary." He dropped the receiver back into its cradle and quickly dressed. Kozol waited by the door for O'Brien. Soon enough, a stocky, middle-aged man with a thick blue parka and beige pants came marching solidly along the outside walkway and knocked on his door. Tony opened it. "Maintenance?"

"O'Brien," said the man, stiffly. "You got a—" he lowered his voice several notches, "rat?"

Tony nodded. "In there. In the tub, at least that's where I left him." Tony stepped outside. It was dark. There were more stars than he had ever seen before. Kozol heard O'Brien say something and he turned. Out of the corner of his eye, Tony noticed the curtain next door again. It had opened and closed ever so slightly.

Some pervert.

As bad as old blue-haired Mrs. Pikipsky, his neighbor back home in the condominium building where he lived with four hundred other lost souls. She was old and cragged enough to have been a cliff dweller once herself. Like the ones Virginia had mentioned to him on the ride to the hotel.

What had she called them? Hohokam? Perhaps that was where all the cliff dwellers had gone. No mystery like Virginia had alluded to. They'd simply retired to condos in south Florida. It was virtually the same thing if you thought about it…

Tony wondered if the Hohokam's homeowners' association had been as bad as his. That alone would be reason enough to abandon a settlement. It was about to drive Kozol out of his own apartment. Perhaps one day anthropologists would discover dozens of empty condo buildings along the south Florida coast. Mysteriously abandoned. Only Tony would know the reason why. O'Brien's cough brought him from his reverie.

"You say something?"

O'Brien stood in the bathroom doorway. "Gotta get something to pick it up with. It'll take me a minute."

Tony didn't want to be left alone with the dead rat for even a minute. "Use the trash can there under the sink," he suggested.

O'Brien turned and seemed to examine the appropriateness of this action. As if a dead rat required some special receptacle or handling. "Yeah," he said finally. "That'll do."

The burly maintenance man scooped the rat from the tub with the plastic trash can and one of Tony's clean towels. Tony was grateful that O'Brien had tossed the towel into the trash bin atop the bloated rat.

Tony moved aside as O'Brien passed through the room with the rat. "Big sucker, ain't it?" the man muttered before departing.

Kozol nodded and watched O'Brien's wide back as he wandered off. The door next to his opened a crack.

"Tony?"

Kozol turned. A bloodshot red eye stared out at him from a darkened room.

"Tony, it's me, John!"

"John?"

The door opened wide. "Come on in," John gestured with his hands. They moved like twin spiders. Beckoning with five spindly legs each.

THREE

THE MAN INSIDE looked nothing like the wild and feckless college student that Tony had once shared a dorm room with.

John's hair was a knotted mess of black quickly being overtaken by gray. His black eyes looked about to burst. Red blood vessels glistened savagely. How could he even see?

John was stooped over. He wore a loose fitting black suit and a wrinkled black dress shirt. His fingers curled and uncurled. Nervously?

"John. You look great," Tony lied. Those short years of lawyering had paid off in dubious social skills. He held out his hand and John, or Janvilhelm shook it vigorously.

"Thanks, man. You too! You too!" John sat on the edge of the bed. "Sit down, man."

Kozol lowered a small blue suitcase from the nearest chair to the floor and sat.

"So, how you doing? Nice place, huh?"

"Yeah, beautiful. You, know, it was a hell of a surprise, you phoning me up from San Francisco. I must have been insane to let you talk me into this though. Not that I don't appreciate the work, John.''

"That's cool, Tony. And take my word for it, the work is easy and the bread is oh-so-good!'' John laughed. "And call me Janvilhelm, okay? That's how all these people know me. Part of the rep—My persona, you know? Janvilhelm Rein Wunderkind, Pianist of the New Age.''

"Sure, John. I mean, Janvilhelm.''

Janvilhelm rose. "Drink?''

"Sure.''

Tony watched as Janvilhelm poured generously from an open bottle of scotch whisky into a couple of hopefully clean bathroom glasses.

"Ice?''

Tony nodded and Janvilhelm tossed a few cubes of ice into Kozol's glass and none into his own.

Janvilhelm raised his glass. "To the New Age,'' he toasted. "May it last forever.''

Tony drank. It was strong, but good quality. Janvilhelm drained his glass in two swift gulps and prepared a refill.

"Are you sure you ought to drink so much?''

Janvilhelm laughed. "Look who's talking,'' he said. "As I remember, you were the one always falling down drunk. I used to have to pick you up!''

"One time," retorted Tony. "I got plastered one damn night after my girlfriend dumped me—what the hell was that girl's name?"

"Barbara."

"Barbara, right. And you keep trotting out that old story like I did nothing but party for four years!"

Janvilhelm sipped his scotch. "Ah, the University of Miami. An undergraduate's playground. The sun, the booze, the women—"

"The women got us in more trouble than the beer," Tony said.

"Amen to that," agreed Janvilhelm. He downed his whiskey. "Another?"

"No, thanks."

"Come on, drink up! It's free. Some fan's been sending me the stuff." John held out the bottle.

Tony shook his head. "I'm still working on this first one."

"Babying it is more like it," chided his friend. "You go over the material?"

"If you mean the CD you sent me, yeah. I hope we get some time to practice. A couple of hours would be nice."

Janvilhelm nodded. "Don't worry, man. I remember what a sharp ear you've got."

"It's been a long time."

Janvilhelm shrugged this off. "You never lose it, man. Never. You'll do just fine tomorrow."

"Some woman named Suzette told me we were performing tonight. Is that true?"

Janvilhelm looked at his gold watch and rubbed his wrist. "Yeah, that's right. Less than a couple of hours until show time. Damn, and I'm hungry. I was hoping we could grab a bite to eat."

"I hear the banquet's at eight."

"Too bad, I was hoping we could go into town and have dinner alone. There's a lot to catch up on, man."

Kozol agreed.

"But I suppose we're obliged. Dr. Kennedy would have a fit if we miss it. The paying guests want to get their money's worth. And that includes mingling with the featured speakers and performers. That's me and you too, Tony. You'll be a celebrity here."

"That's something I could live without," Tony said. "My last pass at celebrity wasn't exactly pleasant."

Janvilhelm grinned like a schoolboy. It made him look ten years younger. Of course, that only made him look closer to his biological age since he was looking pale and old beyond his years. Tony thought the New Age was supposed to be energizing. John-Janvilwelm looked like the New Age was sucking all the energy out of him.

"You mean that murder business? I heard everything worked out okay."

Tony frowned. "Yeah, but being accused of homicide and having your name and face in the newspapers associated with mobsters and murder—" Tony sighed. "That never goes away."

"Sure, it'll pass," Janvilwelm said. "If you let it go, others will."

"That sounds like a New Age truism."

Janvilhelm shrugged and said, "Maybe it is."

"When we talked on the phone, you said that the Florida Bar offered to reinstate your legal license."

"I'm not sure I want to practice law anymore."

"What about that fastfood place? Did you keep it like I said you should?"

Tony shook his head in the negative. "I sold it back to Uncle Jonathan."

"Oh, man!" groaned Janvilhelm. "Are you crazy? That was your meal ticket. I hope you stuck it to him good."

"I sold it back to him for the dollar he charged me for it in the first place."

Janvilhelm groaned again. "Man, are you fucked up!" Now he laughed. And this time it seemed more genuine.

Tony shrugged. "I felt guilty about it. After all, Uncle Jonathan's doing time and Aunt Louise needs all the help she can get, financial and otherwise."

"Well, Mister Nice Guy, money matters. It matters lots." Janvilhelm paused and scratched his cheek. "I've got a twenty-two week tour coming up of the States and the Caribbean. After that, I'll probably do Europe again. I haven't performed there in over three years. My manager says I can get double what I got on the last tour. You're welcome to come. We'll work something out bread-wise, Tony. I could use a guitarist. It fills out the sound and opens up all kinds of other musical avenues for me."

Janvilhelm leaned forward and in a stage whisper said, "I get tired of playing the same old shit. You know what I mean?"

Kozol did. "I know what you mean about the music, but I don't know about the touring, John. I mean, Janvilhelm. I'll have to think about it." It did sound good though. A lot more exciting than practicing law or selling burgers. "Are you sure your Lindi will go along with it?"

"Lindi?"

"Yeah, you know, Lindi Light. I just assumed... Isn't she your manager?"

"Man, where have you been? Me and Lindi

have been split forever. Far as I know that chick has left the planet, Tony boy. I mean, don't get me wrong. Lindi was okay as a manager back when we were doing college bars and frat parties but she couldn't handle the big time. I've got professional management now. The Echo Entertainment Company out of New York. They handle all the bookings." Janvilhelm locked Tony's eyes in a troubling stare. "I don't like to talk about Lindi."

Tony felt uneasy.

Janvilhelm's mood shifted gears once again. One moment friendly, one moment frightening. And Kozol hadn't even asked him why he'd kept peeking out the windows.

"And like I said, the money is fucking great!"

"Let's change the subject," begged Tony.

His friend agreed.

"Who's Dr. Kennedy?"

"Owen Kennedy. Got a doctorate in something or other. He's the dude that organized the Crystal Magic of the Skulls Conference. He has a home here in Sedona, though he travels the New Age circuit quite a bit. Writes books, lectures. You'll meet him tonight if you haven't already."

"No, not yet. Just the girl, Suzette," answered Tony.

"Aristotle, right. Hair black and flowing like liquid sex. Eyes bright blue and mesmerizing."

"Sounds like you know her pretty well—"

"That Suzette," remarked Janvilhelm, "she's a knockout."

"I'll say. A bit odd though."

Janvilhelm laughed raucously. "They're all a bit odd, Tony. Hell, this is the New Age after all! You weren't expecting lawyers in three piece Armani suits with Bruno Magli belts and shoes, were you?" He stuck a slender finger into his empty glass and licked up the drops.

"No, but I've already heard more about crystal skulls and vortexes and energy fields than I ever wanted to know. It's like being in Middle Earth. I'm expecting fairies to pop out from behind the sycamore trees."

"Aliens would be more like it," said Janvilhelm. "Aliens are big among the New Agers. Sedona is like a big intergalactic learning center. Or maybe it's a vacation spot for travelers from other galaxies."

"Like Disney World, but for intelligent beings with pointed ears and green blood?"

"Maybe." Janvilhelm's smile hid enigmatic thoughts. "Did the music make sense to you?"

Tony thought about it. "Yes, it was quite good.

Much different from the rock and roll you used to make up, buddy boy.''

"Things change, Tony. Things change. Attitudes change. Ideas change." He sighed. "Lives change."

"Bingo," echoed Kozol.

There was a rap on the door and Janvilhelm said, "Get that for me, will you?"

"Sure." Tony went for the door while Janvilhelm hastened to the bathroom and shut the door. "Yes?"

A tall, thin, balding man with an impish grin and twinkling green eyes beamed at Kozol. People like that made Tony squeamish, uncomfortable. A quick, deliberate kick to the shin would wipe the grin off the man's face. Tony resisted.

"Hello," said the man. "I was expecting Janvilhelm."

The bathroom door slipped open. "Owen, my man!" Janvilhelm appeared from behind the door and walked deliberately towards Tony and the stranger.

"Janvilhelm!" The two men embraced. "I heard you had checked in. It's not like you to be so seclusive. Are you feeling well?"

"Sure, Owen. A little tired, that's all. Long flight and all that. Tony, this is Dr. Owen Kennedy. I told you about him."

"Pleased to meet you, Dr. Kennedy." Owen Kennedy offered his hand. It was cold, but that could have been due to the temperature outside and not any possible ice in the man's veins. Or alien blood. Tony privately wondered.

"Tony, Tony—"

"Tony Kozol. He's the friend I was telling you about."

"Of course," said Dr. Kennedy. "You are working with Janvilhelm. What an honor it is to have you both."

He shook Tony's hand once more and Kozol stuck his hands in his pockets before the man could do it again.

"I can't tell you how excited everyone is about the concerts you are putting on tonight and again tomorrow evening."

Janvilhelm nodded his head solemnly. "I look forward to working with the crystal skulls. Who knows what magic we might produce."

Tony looked from Janvilhelm to Dr. Kennedy and wondered which man was the crazier.

"Indeed, indeed," said Dr. Kennedy. "The skulls are already in place. Have you seen them, Tony?"

"No, not yet," said Kozol. "I'm looking forward to it though." There were those dubious social skills of his again.

"The skulls are capable of evoking great magic," explained Dr. Kennedy. "Janvilhelm's music is capable of projecting great magic also. I'm sure you are familiar with his use of color and moods to create healing with his music, Mr. Kozol?"

"Yes, of course. And please, call me Tony." Music and colors, wondered Tony, what the hell was the man talking about? Was he talking about the blues? Why didn't he just say so? And did he say healing? Janvilhelm, John, had changed more than Tony had first realized.

Dr. Kennedy looked at his watch. "My goodness. It's all so fascinating. I often forget myself! It's nearly time for the banquet. That's why I had come—to fetch you, Janvilhelm. Shall we?" He looked at the pianist. "Or do you need a few moments to freshen up?"

"Nope, I'm ready. How about you, Tony?"

"I'm afraid what you see is what you get." Dr. Kennedy raised a quizzical eyebrow. "The airline lost my luggage."

"Oh, dear," said Dr. Kennedy. "I'll have the staff check on it if you like. Give me the flight information."

Tony pulled out his ticket and handed it to Dr. Kennedy who put it in his pocket. "Well, we'd

best be going then. Can't be late to our own banquet. I've reserved seats for us at the head table.''

"Actually," said Tony, "I'd sort of made
plans—"

"Nonsense," said Dr. Kennedy. "The featured
guests always sit at the head table."

Janvilhelm grabbed a leather jacket and handed
it to Tony. "Here, you take this, man. It's freezing
out there tonight."

Tony put the jacket on. It was virtually his size.
"Thanks."

THE BANQUET ROOM was filling with guests. It
was a nearly even mixture of men and women,
young and old. Some of the men were formally
attired with brightly polished dress shoes, some in
khakis and polo shirts with loafers despite the
cold, and others wore t-shirts and jeans with
scruffy sneakers. There were several men with po-
nytails and just as many women with closely-
shaved heads. The women in general seemed to
have given a bit more thought to their dress, ca-
sual or otherwise. But then, Tony supposed that
was probably usually the case. A truly eclectic
bunch in any event.

Virginia sat, legs crossed, in an upholstered
beige chair outside the main hall. She rose when
she saw Tony. Her dress was jade green and cut

just low enough in the front to make you wish for more. Her shoes matched. A long brown coat was draped over the back of the chair.

"Hi, Tony. I waited for you. I saved us a couple of seats at a table near the doors. That way, we can sneak out if this thing turns tedious."

Tony noticed a frown pass across the good doctor's face like a swift shadow. "Hi, Virginia," Tony said. "This is Dr. Owen Kennedy and Janvilhelm—"

"—Rein Wunderkind," finished the young woman. "I've heard of you both. Virginia Garner. It's a pleasure."

Dr. Kennedy kissed her hand and Janvilhelm merely fidgeted and mumbled a lame hello.

"I'm afraid I can't join you," began Tony.

"It's my fault, Miss Garner," explained Dr. Kennedy. "Mr. Kozol is required to sit at the head table. It's part of the program. In fact, if you will all excuse me, I see my wife, Camille, calling me to the podium. I've some announcements to make."

Tony shrugged helplessly. "Sorry."

"Oh, that's all right," said Virginia cooly.

"Maybe we can get together after the dinner?"

"We're doing our concert then, Tony," interjected Janvilhelm. "Remember?"

"Oh, right. Well, after that—"

Virginia placed her hand on Kozol's arm. "It's okay, Tony. We'll talk later. I see you at least got a coat. I look forward to hearing you and Janvilhelm perform."

Inside the ballroom, Dr. Kennedy called for everyone to be seated. Dinner was on a tight schedule, he explained, with the concert and reception to follow shortly thereafter, with a cash bar.

Janvilhelm grabbed Tony by the neck and gently pushed him inside. Kozol looked back one more time but Virginia had already moved to her seat and was making conversation with a gentleman to her left.

Tony was seated next to some woman named Annie Campbell on his right and his friend, Janvilhelm to the left. Next to Janvilhelm sat Suzette Aristotle who greeted Tony Kozol warmly when he approached. Beside her sat Dr. Kennedy and his wife, Camille. Janvilhelm had neglected to tell Kozol what a looker the doctor's wife was herself.

Camille Kennedy possessed silky, straight blonde hair that fell to the middle of her back and pale blue eyes. She had strong Nordic features and sat silently while her husband talked. There was a look of smouldering rapture about her. That was the only way Tony could describe it to himself.

Mrs. Kennedy wore a clingy black catsuit with a short leopard skin stole. Kozol wondered if it was fake. She looked a bit like a girl Tony knew back home, only more rounded. There were three others at the table whom Tony had been introduced to but whose names he had promptly forgotten.

The waiter stuck a plate in front of him. Dinner was apparently seafood. Snapper by the look of it. Covered in brightly colored chopped bits of red, green and yellow which Kozol assumed were vegetable and edible. In the end it didn't matter, Tony ate. He was starving.

Annie interrupted his chewing. "And what is it that you are here for, Mr. Kozol? I hadn't noticed your name in the program."

Tony nodded and swallowed. "Not in it," he explained. "Janvilhelm asked me to come at the last minute to fill in for another accompanist who took sick."

"Ah, a musician. How interesting."

"Not really. I mean, music is interesting. It's that I'm not really a musician."

Miss Campbell smiled. She appeared approximately forty-five, maybe fifty years old. She barely touched her food. Perhaps that was why the woman was so thin. She wore her wavy brown hair short. If she pulled, her hair might reach her chin, but no further. She was bundled in a warm looking, dark purple sweater and black skirt. Miss Campbell's face was nearly as pale as the linen. "You're here in Sedona to play music. You're a musician."

Tony shrugged. "I suppose. And you?"

Annie Campbell put down her fork. "I am a psychic and a channeler."

Tony's face must have betrayed his lack of understanding for Miss Campbell continued.

"I channel spirits."

"You mean the dead?" Tony was naive but he certainly had seen a movie or two where the psychic channels the spirit of long dead Uncle Chester or some such person.

"More like the alien."

"Alien?"

"Yes. It strikes you odd?" She was grinning. "I don't mind. Many don't understand. I'm giving a lecture tomorrow and a workshop on Sunday. You should come."

"I'll try," said Tony. What the hell, it could be fun, if not downright funny. "What sort of aliens do you channel?"

"It's not a sort, it is a race. They call themselves the Ramadians."

Tony laughed. "Ramada Inns? It sounds like a hotel!"

Annie giggled good-naturedly in return. "No, no. Ramadians," she said slowly. "They are from Proxima Centauri in the celestial Southern Hemisphere."

"I'm from Ocean Palm, myself," said Tony. "That's in south Florida."

Annie said patiently, "You are a skeptic, aren't you?"

Tony grinned and picked at an asparagus tip on his plate. "How could you tell?"

"Proxima Centauri is the closest star to our own solar system. A red dwarf in the constellation Centaurus. Its orbit is said to take about a million of our Earth years. To the Ramadians it is but the blink of the eye."

Tony raised an eyebrow. There was nothing much to say in response.

"They are an ancient and long-lived race."

Suzette spoke up. "According to legend, Tony, the Ramadians have visited Earth many times. The crystal skulls are a manifestation of such visits. The early peoples whom they visited were instructed to carve these crystal skulls into which the Ramadians placed knowledge. Knowledge which we were unable to understand or use in those times."

"Indeed," interjected Dr. Owen Kennedy.

"The early humans were instructed to bury these skulls—"

"Like Mork and Mindy?" Kozol asked.

"Maggie and Azul," corrected Suzette.

"—for future generations to uncover and, hopefully," Dr. Kennedy said with a tone of mystery, "reveal the knowledge and wisdom within."

Janvilhelm began humming the theme to the old Twilight Zone t.v. show. "Come on, now, gang. Let's give the new guy a break. I'd like him to stick around a while. You're spooking him!"

"Yes, let's definitely keep him around a while." Suzette gave Tony a warm look. "By the way, Tony, I sent a shopper into town for you. To pick up a few things. Pants, underwear, socks, shirts."

Tony groaned. "Really, you needn't have done that, Miss Aristotle." He sensed his face commuting to an embarrassing shade of red. "I'm sure the airline will find my stuff."

"Sooner or later," guessed Janvilhelm. "They once lost a keyboard of mine and it ended up in South Africa instead of South Carolina!"

"Well, thanks anyway. I'll pay you back."

Suzette waved Kozol off. "It was nothing. Perhaps, if it makes you feel better, I'll let you buy me dinner sometime."

"Sure," said Tony. "It's a deal."

"Sounds like a date to me," Janvilhelm apparently couldn't help but jest. He turned to Suzette. "I've known you for a long time, Suzette. And now I find out that all I had to do was toss all my clothes and blame it on the airlines to get a date with you!"

Suzette shrugged. "You see how easy it is." She looked past Janvilhelm. "How about tomorrow evening then, Tony?"

"Oh, a-alright."

Janvilhelm gave Tony a collegiate pat on the back. "I've said it before and I'll say it again, Suzette," began Janvilhelm as he rose unsteadily to his feet, the effects of the whiskey and more than his share of wine with dinner having taking their heady toll, "you look so familiar... somehow...you remind me of someone...more and more..."

The New Age pianist gazed cryptically at Suzette Aristotle as if the answer would be written on her beautiful face. "Somehow. Perhaps another life..."

Suzette only shook her head, her dark lips curled in a frown.

Janvilhelm scratched his unshaven chin and said to his old roommate, "Come on, Tony, my boy. Let's warm up the old chops."

With a nod, Janvilhelm bid goodbye to the oth-

ers at the table. Tony rose and followed. After all,
Janvilhelm was paying the bills. And Tony's
chops could use all the warming up he could get.
He hadn't performed in public for years!

A DEAD RAT dangled from the door handle of Janvilhelm's room. It had been attached by a dirty
white shoelace, one end around the doorknob, the
other around the beast's neck.

Janvilhelm looked quickly over his shoulder
then back to the rat. He held it up by the shoe-
string. "What do you think, Tony?"

"I don't think it looks like a suicide, if that's
what you're asking, John."

Janvilhelm pulled a pocketknife from his trousers, cut the string and hurled the rat into the darkness of the cold, arid desert. "Lots of nuts out
there, man. Probably some wacko who doesn't
like my music." The end of the shoelace dangled
like a message of death from the brass doorknob.
Janvilhelm stuck in his hotel keycard and held the
door open for Tony. "Just got to grab my bag.
You need anything?"

"My guitar. It's in my room."

Janvilhelm picked up a black gig bag. "Let's
get it and set up in the conference room for a
sound check."

Tony grabbed his guitar and they headed back

towards the main building. "You know, I had a rat in my room tonight also— It was in the tub."

"Really? Must've been meant for me. I had the hotel swap our rooms. 405 is a bad number for me."

"And you're not concerned?"

Janvilhelm paused and looked back down the hill towards the wing of the resort where their rooms were located. "Nah, it's probably nothing. You'd be surprised how many nuts there are chasing you around when you're a celebrity, even a minor one like me," he said in a self-deprecating tone.

"Maybe you should notify the hotel?"

Janvilhelm laughed. "That there was a rat on my door? Not worth the time. Could be there's a rat infestation. Besides, this has been happening for a couple of months now. Just about everywhere I go a dead rat shows up."

"Aren't you worried?"

"If I were a rat I'd be worried."

"But still—"

"Look," said Janvilhelm, "I expect it's some nutty groupie. Probably some chick I slept with one night who just can't get over me!"

Janvilhelm's laugh wasn't real, suspected Tony. "Anyone in particular?"

"Well now, there have been more than a few,

my boy. And with so many of the same people going from one conference to another, it's hard to say.''

"I still can't believe you're into all this. You never showed any interest in the New Age back when we were in college."

"No, I suppose not. That's Lindi's influence, I guess. She was into all that shit, remember? Wanted to call our band the Tarotheads!"

"I do remember," said Tony. "She even did my astrological chart when we met. Told me I was going to be a successful attorney."

"Probably trying to make you feel good. Or maybe she meant that you were going to *need* a successful attorney."

"Very funny." The two men stood outside Mystic Hall. "You ever try to contact her?"

"Never," said Janvilhelm, "I haven't. And I wouldn't know where to begin. Besides, the past is the past. Dead and buried. Like I said before, things change. I mean, do you ever think about looking up that ex-fiancée of yours?" Janvilhelm lifted the top of the piano and placed the brace. He plucked a string.

"No," said Tony, surprised that even the thought of his own former lover could still evoke such emotion. "Let's play."

Janvilhelm grinned. "I thought you'd never

ask.'' He sat at the satin black piano, closed his eyes, tilted his neck back and let his fingers touch the keys. "Spring Colors," he said, "in G major."

Kozol lifted his guitar from its case and played along. Tony had to admit, the music itself was lifting. They played through several instrumentals on the latest Janvilhelm Rein Wunderkind CD, "Moods for all Seasons."

"This is what it's all about," said Janvilhelm, as they paused. "The music. The muse."

The sound of two hands clapping came from the rear staff entrance to the hall. "Beautiful," cooed Suzette. "Truly beautiful. And you," she said, pressing Tony's arm, "you are quite good."

"Thanks."

"The new album is doing well?"

Janvilhelm shrugged modestly. "Number two on the New Age charts this week and last. Fifty-thousand units in three months."

"Wow," said Tony. "I had no idea."

"It's not like the Rolling Stones but it sells. And I own my own label and merchandising."

"How much are you paying me again?" Tony joked.

"Enough!" shot back Janvilhelm quickly. "So what's up, Suzette?"

"I've brought Maggie and Azul." She had her

hand wrapped tightly around the handle of a gray aluminum case that was about the same size as a cat carrier. Suzette opened the case with a tiny silver key she wore on a chain around her neck. First Suzette removed a black silk cloth which she placed over the empty table center stage. Next she stood two Plexiglas stands one beside the other near the middle.

And finally, as Tony watched with great interest, she removed the two crystal skulls, Maggie and Azul, from their home and placed them carefully on their stands.

Suzette mumbled an inaudible prayer or message of some sort, one hand atop each skull, then turned and looked at the two musicians with satisfaction. "Maggie and Azul say they are comfortable. This place is acceptable to them."

Janvilhelm jumped up from the piano bench. "Great! I need a drink." He massaged his fingers. "We'll be at the bar. Call me when it's showtime, Suzette. Come on, Tony."

ANNIE CAMPBELL was called up to the stage by Dr. Owen Kennedy and, after what seemed an interminable introduction, she sat at the table and solemnly studied the crystal skulls. Suzette crept slowly away.

Janvilhelm struck an A minor chord on the piano

with his left hand and followed with a rapid arpeggio using his right. "It's showtime!"

Tony gazed at the skulls. The engineer manning the console in the back of the room aimed twin beams of red laser lights at Maggie and Azul. The beams cut across the room like they were living creatures of light. Perhaps drawn to beings similar. The two crystal skulls seemed to throb and blink.

The room began to fill and Tony took his place beside Janvilhelm, but his eyes never left the skulls.

The room lights dimmed and Dr. Kennedy approached the podium. "My friends…" he began solemnly. Tony shut out the doctor's ineloquent words.

Then, after a mercifully brief introduction, Suzette Aristotle, looking striking in a long, midnight blue gown that magnified the blueness of her eyes, rose and ascended the stage. All lights were out, but for the red beams projected from the rear of the hall. "Good evening, my friends, my fellow travelers. This evening we are blessed. The wonderful Janvilhelm Rein Wunderkind and his special guest, guitarist extraordinaire, Tony Kozol, will arouse and enlighten us—"

Janvilhelm passed Tony a decidedly lecherous grin.

"—with their extraterrestrial musings which I shall humbly try to facilitate towards communication with Magdalena and Azultican, our Ramadian guests." She turned to Miss Campbell. "And we are doubly fortunate to have Miss Annie Campbell here to translate for us the energies of Maggie and Azul. Annie," Suzette said with a studious bow, "we are honored." Suzette left the stage and took a seat in the front row beside Chief Howling Wind.

All eyes focused on Annie Campbell, Janvilhelm Rein Wunderkind and Tony himself. But mostly they focused on Maggie and Azul.

For several moments Annie said nothing. Her eyes were tightly shut. Red light played across the skulls like liquid energy. Her hands each touched a skull, her right Maggie, her left Azul.

Without opening her eyes, Annie nodded. That was their cue. Janvilhelm began playing. A light projector began beaming hues of blue, green and red across a tall white screen which had been set up behind the grand piano. Tony gazed at the images of color, mesmerized, while his fingers moved effortlessly across the frets.

As his eyes grew accustomed to the darkness, Kozol spotted Virginia. She was seated with that man again, the one he had seen her talking to at

the banquet. Why did that bother him? He decided
it shouldn't.

A rising wail began to emanate from the table.
Tony turned and realized that Annie Campbell,
self-proclaimed alien channeler, was chanting. It
sounded like a female wolf giving birth. Perhaps
a little alien would pop out from her loins!

If aliens ever did show up on Earth, Tony
wasn't quite certain which would be the stranger,
the aliens or the New Agers. Surely if he were
still an attorney and had any of this bunch for a
client up on murder charges, an insanity plea
would be a safe bet.

As the show ended and the lights came up, Dr.
Kennedy thanked everyone for their participation
with thunderous applause playing in the background, while rolling portable bars were set up at
opposite ends of Mystic Hall and the drinks began
to flow.

Janvilhelm crossed behind Tony and hugged
Annie. "Nice act," he commented.

"The only acting I do is smiling when you're
around," Annie countered.

Suzette returned to the stage and began packing
up Maggie and Azul in their aluminum traveling
case.

"Ooh, feeling wicked. I like that."

"Screw you, Janvilhelm."

"My room, eleven o'clock."

"I'd rather be dead."

"When you're having sex, who can tell the difference?!"

Annie Campbell looked like she was about to slap him. But before she could, Janvilhelm laughed, turned and proceeded towards the nearest open bar.

"Sorry," said Tony, though he wasn't sure what he was apologizing for. "I think he's stressed out— Plus, he's been drinking heavily all evening. When he drinks, Janvilhelm can be a bit of a—"

"Rat?"

"I was thinking pig," said Kozol.

"Yes, a pig," mused Miss Campbell. "Why didn't I think of that. A fat, greedy little pig..."

Tony looked surprised. "Excuse me?"

"Nothing," Annie said. Her smile was broad and she seemed self-satisfied. As if she knew a secret that the world did not. "Shall we have a drink?"

Tony nodded and they headed through the crowd, stopping often as members of the audience congratulated the two of them on the evening's remarkable performance. It seemed many of them had felt a communion with the skulls and even the Ramadians themselves. Tony, feeling generous in his assessment of humanity at that moment, felt that the thin mountain air had affected their thinking capacity.

Kozol noticed Virginia grabbing hold of Janvilhelm and pointing in their direction. Janvilhelm, a tumbler of scotch balanced in one hand, made a face and pushed her off. "Excuse me," Tony said. "I'd better check on Janvilhelm."

"Don't be his patsy, Tony. Stay." Her hand rested on his shoulder.

"He's my friend. I'll be right back."

Annie said sharply, "Janvilhelm has a way of using his friends."

Kozol shrugged helplessly and fought his way through the tight crowd. Out of the corner of his eye, Tony caught a glimpse of Virginia slipping on her coat and making her way out. Janvilhelm was now regaling a pair of elderly women with his wit or his drunken stupor. In either case, he seemed reasonably contented now.

Janvilhelm called to Tony from across the room. Even from a distance, his bloodshot eyes stood out and he wobbled noticeably on his feet. "Forget the redhead, Tony! She's all wet— I told her to go soak herself!"

Kozol ignored Janvilhelm's remarks and decided to follow Virginia. The crowd was thinnest nearest the door but there was no sign of the girl in the hall or the lobby. Tony hit the bell on the counter as the desk was deserted. Mark entered from the back office. Didn't he ever sleep? Or even go home?

"May I help you?" the assistant manager asked. "Ah, our Mr. Kozol." He reached behind the counter. "I've a package for you." He lifted a paper sack with the name of a local department store printed on its side and set it on the counter.

Tony peeked inside. Clothes and shoes. "Thanks. This must be from—" Tony stopped. There was no point in telling Mark who had bought him the gear. "Did you see a pretty redhead go by?"

Mark shook his head no.

"She was dressed in green—"

"No," said Mark slowly. "Apparently she's outrun you. And you— Have you seen any more rats, sir?"

"As a matter of fact, I have. Hanging by a shoelace from a door handle!"

Mark responded with a patronizing grin, "Perhaps he was despondent that the market for cheese had collapsed. I hear the rats were quite bullish on it."

"Perhaps," replied Tony, "it was the poor quality of room service."

Mark smirked. "Perhaps it was the poor quality of his roommate."

Tony grabbed his bag of clothes and left. There was nothing worse than a wiseass. Especially when he was funnier than you.

Tony's room was dark. The walkway outside his room was dark also. "The bulbs must be out," muttered Tony, as he fumbled, cold and tired, for his room key. A crash came from next door. That was Janvilhelm's room! He put an ear to the door. Nothing. He knocked.

The door flew open and a dark figure ran past him, hopped over the stones and sprinted across the parking lot. Tony hesitated for only a moment and then took off in pursuit. Of what or who he didn't know.

It didn't matter.

Away from the lights of the resort, he was soon surrounded by inky darkness. He heard steps running in the distance. But there was no telling exactly which direction they followed. He hadn't even been able to make out if it was a man or a woman he was chasing. It was too fast, too dark. Hell, it could have been a Ramadian for all he knew.

And in the darkness, Tony was afraid he'd either get lost, run into a cactus, a hungry coyote, or even worse fall down some lousy cliff. The damn place was probably full of them. Kozol slowed to a stop.

Besides, what was he running for? Did he really want to catch up to some burglar? The landscape was cold, dark and silent. All of a sudden, red rock country wasn't looking so inviting.

Kozol turned and followed the glow of manmade light back to the rooms. Janvilhelm's door stood wide. Tony entered and took a quick look around. There was nothing missing so far as he could tell and the lock wasn't broken. It was only a hotel room after all. Who'd want to steal that cookie cutter shit?

Tony shut the door firmly and retired to his own room. He'd report the break-in in the morning. Let Janvilhelm deal with it. No point reporting it tonight.

Not with Mark on duty.

Kozol cranked up the heat to stave off the ever present chill and collapsed into bed. The hell with them all. The hell with Virginia, the hell with Suzette and the hell with John! He fell asleep with visions of aliens with crystal skulls having sex with wolves at Ramada Inns.

A frightful whirring noise woke him. It was the telephone. He picked up the receiver. "Hello?" A low, muffled voice responded. It sounded like Janvilhelm. He sounded drunk and it sounded like he said Mystic Hall. The phone went dead. Tony sat up and looked at the clock-radio beside the bed. It was three a.m. "Oh, shit."

Kozol flopped back down on his pillow, his head falling like a watermelon in freefall. He fell asleep, then woke again with a start. The clock radio now read 3:15.

Tony groaned, rolled out of bed and pulled on his pants and shoes. He'd never taken off his shirt. Kozol grabbed Janvilhelm's leather jacket from the desk chair where he'd tossed it, and stepped next door. Janvilhelm's room was dark but that wasn't surprising. He tried knocking. No response.

Tony sighed and headed for the main building. It sounded like Janvilhelm was going to need some sobering up and it wouldn't be the first time. Janvilhelm was right, Tony was thinking as he entered the unlocked, yet deserted lobby, some things never change.

The Red Rock Resort was bathed in low yellow light. A smouldering fire lingered in the fireplace. The place was quiet as a mausoleum. At least there was no sign of Mark. Probably asleep in the back, or out trapping rats for tomorrow's new arrivals.

Tony pulled open one of the big doors to Mystic Hall. The lights were off but for a beam of red light aiming at the stage. Janvilhelm sat at the piano.

Rather, the grand piano pretty much sat on him. The upper half of Janvilhelm's body had been all but swallowed by the cover of the piano.

Limp.

Kozol approached slowly. "Janvilhelm?" he whispered, in trembling tones. Was it the cold of Sedona or the apparent coldness of his friend, Janvilhelm? Tony touched Janvilhelm's sleeve. "John?"

Still no answer.

Shaking, Tony raised the heavy lid of the piano. It took some effort. He hissed when he saw the splash of blood that engulfed Janvilhelm's skull and spattered the inside of the piano itself. "Damn."

FOUR

SLOWLY, FIGHTING THE URGE to throw up, Tony began to return the piano lid to its original position.

But he stopped halfway.

Kozol couldn't bear the thought of it resting atop Janvilhelm's crushed skull any longer. Tony grabbed the bar that held the piano open and braced the lid in the upright position.

Kozol took a deep breath. He'd have to report the accident. Tony turned and hesitated. It didn't seem right leaving Janvilhelm there. But then again, where was the guy going to go?

The voice seemed to boom from across the hall. "I suggest you stay where you are, Mr. Kozol!"

Tony jumped and turned around. Mark stood at the far door staring menacingly in his direction.

"I've telephoned the police and an ambulance. They should all be here shortly."

"There-there's been an accident—" began Tony. He paced towards Mark.

Mark stepped back and said, "Please stay where you are, Mr. Kozol. We'll let the police sort this out."

"But you don't think—" Tony looked at Janvilhelm. Kozol sighed and hoped that Janvilhelm wasn't really dead.

But he was.

There had been an uncomfortable silence as the two men stood waiting for help to turn up. The police arrived first. With no sirens. Probably out of deference to the sleeping guests. A uniformed officer said good morning to Mark and proceeded to inspect Janvilhelm.

He ignored Tony.

The officer felt for a pulse. "Nothing." He spoke a few words into the radio clipped to his shirt. "Ambulance will be here shortly," he said to the assistant manager. "They're just leaving the medical center now."

Mark nodded.

A BURLY MAN and an even burlier woman arrived ten minutes later. "Oh, Christ," grumbled the man, "better get the gurney."

"I got it last time!"

"Just get it, Marge," he complained. "Please?" He pushed the side of a black moustache out of his thick mouth and inspected either the piano or Janvilhelm. Kozol couldn't really tell which. "Nice."

"Can't move him yet, Ron. Gotta wait for the

team to get here. And they ain't gonna be happy being driven from their beds at this hour." The officer glanced at his watch. "Where are you going?" he shouted.

Kozol froze. "I'm exhausted. I thought I'd go back to my room."

"You found the body, right?"

Kozol nodded.

The officer aimed his index finger towards the first row of chairs. "Sit."

Tony sat. He woke with a lady in a brown suit poking him in the shoulder. "Huh?"

"Mr. Kozol?"

Tony yawned and squeezed his eyes. "What time is it?"

"Five-thirty. Let's get some coffee and talk."

Tony followed the woman in the brown suit to the lobby where a fresh pot of coffee and a tray of muffins was installed on a nearby sideboard. They helped themselves and sat at a small table overlooking the resort's par three golf course.

"I'm Detective Gibson, Sedona Police. I need to ask you a few questions."

"Sure," agreed Tony, rubbing his face. It felt like scratchy putty and he needed to pee.

The detective laid a don't-fuck-with-me-or-I'll-toss-your-ass-in-jail look on Tony— A look he knew only too well from the time he'd been accused of murder in Florida—and said, "So, the assistant manager, Mark Taggert, is out making his rounds and says he finds you standing over the body. That right?"

"Yeah."

"You a friend of the deceased?"

"Yes. That is, we were friends in college. After that…" Tony sipped his coffee. It was bitter and he added another packet of sugar.

"After that, what?"

Tony studied the detective. She had brown hair cut short around the ears. It was the same shade as his own, or nearly so. With brown eyes and a no nonsense demeanor. If she wore any makeup at all it was impossible to tell.

Finally he said, "You know how it is. We lost touch. Not completely. We still talked once in a while. Exchanged a few letters. That was about it until he called me for this job."

"Know anybody who'd want to kill him?"

"No." Tony sat up taller. "You're thinking murder? What makes you think somebody would want to kill him?"

"Funny way to commit suicide—dropping a piano lid on your skull. There are easier ways."

"Maybe it was an accident." Tony gave up on the muffin. Pulling it apart reminded him too much of Janvilhelm's own split skull in the other room. "John had been drinking. He's sitting at the piano and leans over for some reason...not really paying attention, and accidently hits the bar holding up the lid—"

"Maybe." Detective Gibson fumbled in her pockets and finally pulled a roll of candy from her inside coat pocket. She cut through the paper with a short, sharp fingernail, ignoring the string that was made for the purpose, and tossed a peppermint Lifesaver into her coffee.

The detective stirred it around with her finger. Apparently she wasn't pain-sensitive. "So, tell me what you were doing in Mystic Hall at three in the morning? Piano practice?"

Tony leaned back, his hands clutching the edge of the table, reliving those moments in his mind. It already seemed like ages ago, instead of hours... He shook his head no as the detective proffered a candy. "I got a phone call," he explained.

"From the victim?"

"Yeah, I mean it sounded like him." Tony paused. "Yeah, I'm sure it was him. He sounded really drunk though, like I told you, you know?"

"Autopsy will tell us," Det. Gibson said dispassionately. "So, Janvilhelm calls you—"

Tony nodded. "Like I said, John sounded drunk. Said something about needing a lawyer and—'' Tony tried to remember John's exact words, but he was so tired. "I don't know, he might have said something else but he was wasted and I was half asleep.''

The detective gave Kozol a sour, reproachful look. What did she expect? How could he have known that his friend would end up dead? Possibly murdered...

"And then he said something about meeting him in Mystic Hall.''

"So you came.''

"That's right. Well,'' Tony explained, "I fell asleep— Just for a minute or two. Then I got dressed and came down here.'' Kozol's voice grew quiet. If only he had come sooner... If only he hadn't fallen back to sleep... Tony looked towards Mystic Hall. "That's when I found John.''

"Or killed him.''

"Found him.''

Det. Gibson frowned ambivalently.

"Are you actually accusing me?'' His voice rose above the quiet sounds of morning.

"I'm asking you,'' she replied, apparently immune to his shouting. "Did you kill him?''

Tony rose. "Screw you.''

The detective grinned. "I'm afraid you're not my type, Kozol.''

"I'm not sure you even have a blood type, let alone a sex type."

A storm brewed in Gibson's eyes. "Sit down, wiseass."

Kozol sat. The two glared at each other across the tiny table. The room was quiet and empty but for Tony and the detective, and the crackling of the fire, a soft reminder that sooner or later all are consumed.

"What are you so uppity about?" asked Det. Gibson, finally. "What have you got to hide?"

"Nothing." Tony hunched over and wrapped his hands around his coffee cup.

"My problem is you could be lying about the phone call. You were found standing over the body. The manager found you—"

"Assistant manager," interjected Kozol. He couldn't bear Mark getting more credit or recognition than he deserved.

She shrugged and went on. "And Janvilhelm is sitting there dead at his piano bench while you conveniently claim to have found his body. You ever do any acting, Mr. Kozol?"

"This is getting dreary, detective..." Tony squeezed a muffin in his fingers, releasing the scent of bananas and nuts.

"Did I mention I heard some interesting things about you from the police in Ocean Palm?"

"No, you didn't."

"Very interesting." She popped another Lifesaver and rolled it around inside her mouth.

"I'll bet."

"Said you were involved in a murder— Some homeless guy and a well-known gangster."

"Involved? Entangled is more like it. My uncle pretty much got me into that mess."

"Yeah, I know. A Detective Fender explained the case to me. Quite an adventure, eh?"

Tony waited. Det. Gibson seemed to have her own agenda and he didn't feel like helping her along with it.

"You were a lawyer."

"Is that a crime?"

Det. Gibson smiled. She looked almost human then, in an edgy sort of way. "No, I just wondered how you came to be playing guitar at a New Age conference. Quite a career change."

"Seemed like a good time for one," Tony commented.

Det. Gibson laughed out loud. "It might be time for one again!"

"What's that supposed to mean?" Kozol's voice was weary and not a little defensive.

"Relax, Mr. Kozol. I only meant that with your employer dead you may want to think about your next career move."

"Oh, right." Tony looked over his shoulder towards Mystic Hall. The stretcher was being rolled silently away now by Burly and Burlier. Janvilhelm passed but Kozol couldn't see his face through the body bag. "Damn."

Det. Gibson rose and told Tony to go and get some rest. Which is exactly what he intended to do when Mark called to him from behind the front desk. Mark, the assistant manager, looked as tired as Kozol felt.

"What is it now?" asked Tony.

Mark held up a key card. "I'm afraid the police have sealed off your room, Mr. Wunderkind's as well."

"Oh, great."

"That reminds me. I caught someone running out of John's room last night."

"What time was that?" asked Det. Gibson.

Kozol shrugged. "Around eleven, I guess."

"Did you report it?"

Mark huffed. "No, he did not."

"I was going to this morning—"

"Never mind." The detective folded her arms across her chest. "We'll check it out."

"And what am I supposed to do?"

"I've another room all set up for you. Fortunately we had a cancellation last night. The hotel is rather full."

"Not as full as it used to be," remarked Tony, with a nod towards Mystic Hall.

"Indeed," said Mark. "I've had your things, that is, your bag of clothes sent over to the new room."

"What?!" barked Det. Gibson. "You can't go—"

The assistant manager stopped her short. "Don't worry, detective. One of your officers searched the bag first. Not much to see. A lady friend bought Mr. Kozol some new underwear."

Det. Gibson smirked. "You're a class act, aren't you, Kozol?"

Tony grabbed the keycard from Mark's hand. Kozol's next remark was cut off as Suzette Aristotle came running wildly into the lobby screaming. She was dressed in a pale blue jogging suit and neat white sneakers and carrying on like a madwoman. And still she looked sexier than most women could in a formal ball gown discretely discussing politics at some fancy social function. Her hair was tied back with one of those thingamajigs. A white one.

"They're gone! My god, they're gone!" She looked at Mark and then turned to Tony and grabbed him by the coat.

Tony tried to calm her down. "Relax, relax. Who's gone?"

"Maggie and Azul— They're missing!" A tiny rivulet of sweat rolled down from the side of her temple and snuck under her chin.

Tony watched it, admiring its glistening trail across her smooth cheek. "Maybe the aliens snatched them off to Arcturus. Or maybe Azul and Maggie have spirited themselves off to some hidden vortex in the hills seeking mystic guidance."

Suzette sniffled. "And here I thought you would care. But-but you're as insensitive as-as a rock…"

Kozol sighed. "I'm sorry, Suzette." She hugged him now. Her breath was warm and her cheek was cold against his own. He smelled the same perfume in her hair as he had the day he'd met her.

"What's going on here?"

Tony pulled Suzette off of himself and turned. It was Det. Gibson.

"Who are you?" demanded Suzette, suddenly seeming to regain considerably her composure. She flicked an errant lock of hair from her face.

"Det. Gibson, Sedona P.D. And you are?" The detective bit her lower lip and chewed.

"Oh, the police. Thank goodness. Maggie and Azul are missing."

"Maggie and—" Det. Gibson hesitated, "Azul?"

Suzette nodded and sniffed. "Yes, I'm sorry if I seem so upset. But they're my children after all…"

Det. Gibson gently took Suzette by the arm. "I understand. Tell me what happened. Would you care to sit, Miss—"

"Aristotle. Suzette Aristotle. I think I should stand. I'm too anxious to sit."

"I understand." Det. Gibson nodded compassionately. "Now tell me what's happened."

"Well, I'd gotten up early to go jogging. I'd left Maggie and Azul in the room. They were sleeping after all. I wasn't gone, oh, thirty or forty minutes— I only ran around the grounds a couple of times and when I came back, they were gone!"

Tony was rolling his eyes. "Det. Gibson—"

"Not now, Mr. Kozol," she said sharply.

"But, Det. Gibson—"

"Stop interrupting, Mr. Kozol. I thought I told you to go and get some rest."

"Suddenly I'm not feeling so tired."

Det. Gibson gifted Tony with an icy stare. "Then I suggest you keep your mouth shut."

Tony threw his hands in the air and leaned against the front desk with Mark, the assistant manager, who hung on every word being said.

"Miss Aristotle, you know you really should not be leaving your children alone in a hotel room, even if they are sleeping."

"I know," Suzette replied, "I don't like to do it. But I have to get out sometimes. I have to have some life outside of them."

Det. Gibson looked unimpressed with Suzette's logic. "What are the children's ages?" She took a tattered notepad from her breast pocket.

"Oh, my. We're not sure you know. We've had them tested, of course, by several experts. Maggie could be anywhere from two thousand to eight thousand years old. Azul claims to be younger."

Tony snickered. He couldn't help it. Det. Gibson gave him a glare that cut him cold.

"Perhaps you are in shock, Miss Aristotle. Would you care for some coffee?" Suzette nodded and Det. Gibson said, "Please get some coffee and something to eat for Miss Aristotle, Mark."

Mark nodded and silently went to the sideboard.

"Det. Gibson," said Suzette, "do you think you'll be able to find Maggie and Azul quickly? They're quite valuable. Besides, everyone is expecting to see them this afternoon."

"How's that?" Det. Gibson took the mug of coffee from Mark and handed it to the victim.

"There is a feature presentation of the skulls taking place at one o'clock, in Mystic Hall. The skulls are the main attraction."

"In the first place," said the detective, "I wouldn't be expecting anything to take place in Mystic Hall. Not today, and probably not tomorrow. And in the second place, what exactly do your kids have to do with these skulls you're talking about? Your kids' skulls some kind of attraction?"

Tony held his breath.

"My kids? Oh, no," said Suzette between sips of black coffee. She managed a grin. "You misunderstand. Maggie and Azul are my children in a cosmic sense. Magic crystal skulls which the Ramadians have been purported to have infused with the wisdom of their race."

Det. Gibson spoke through gritted teeth. "These aren't people?"

"Of course not. Don't be ridiculous. They aren't people at all. At least, not in a human sense."

Det. Gibson looked ready to explode. "Maggie and Azul, they're not people, they're skulls?"

"Yes."

"Not human skulls?"

"No."

"Crystal skulls?"

"Yes. I've a picture of them right here." Suzette fumbled around in her purse and pulled out a wrinkled conference brochure. She offered it to the detective. Magdalena and Azultican were featured prominently on the pink cover.

Det. Gibson took it from Suzette with barely a glance. The detective crumbled the flyer in her fine bony fingers, nodded slowly, ominously. "Miss Aristotle," she said grimly, "would you mind waiting for me in Mystic Hall. Back of the room, please. Officer Grunwald will keep you company. In fact, you can give him the details." The Sedona detective turned to Tony now, but her words were for Miss Aristotle. "I'll be there shortly."

"Of course," replied Suzette.

Tony watched Suzette's backside with growing appreciation. But then, he'd have rather stared at an elephant's hemorrhoidal backside than look into Det. Gibson's eyes at that moment.

"You knew?" Det. Gibson said.

Tony nodded.

"And you didn't tell me—"

"You didn't give me the chance!" Tony looked around for Mark in case he needed backup. But Mark had conveniently disappeared into the woodwork once again.

"I ought to arrest you!"

"For what?" Tony shouted back.

"For making me look like a-a—"

"Numbskull?" Tony suggested, filling in the blank.

Det. Gibson turned on her sturdy, low heels and left in the direction of the now deadly Mystic Hall.

Kozol grinned in satisfaction. Finally he'd found someone he could one up. And it felt good.

Real good.

FIVE

"Hey!"

Tony waved and shouted towards Virginia, who stood in the lobby, dressed casually in jeans and jacket. She had a tiny blue knapsack on her back. He was wearing the new clothes Suzette had purchased for him. Amazingly, they fit. That girl had an eye for detail.

"Hello." Virginia spoke, then turned her attention back to the man she'd been speaking with— a staffer who was explaining the differences between several of the local Jeep tours. The name Wilbur was stitched in red letters to the man's white shirt.

Kozol sensed her coolness. "Virginia, I'm sorry I missed you last night."

"Sure," replied Virginia stiffly. "How about this tour?" With her thumb she pointed to a section of the brochure she'd been perusing. "It says the guides are very experienced and include an in-depth history of the local, indigenous tribes as well as geological background—two hours and forty-five minutes— Is it any good?" she asked the elderly assistant. "Will this take me to some of the out of the way spots?"

Wilbur nodded as if he appreciated her choice. "The Mystery Tour Company. One of the best tours around for the money. Not so touristy, if you know what I mean."

Virginia said she did.

Wilbur looked at his silver watch. "I've got one of their Jeeps scheduled for eleven-thirty. Party of three. I expect they'll be here anytime. There's room for more, if you'd like to take it."

"How much?"

"Fifty-five."

"All right," said Virginia. "That sounds fine." She pulled her wallet out of her knapsack and removed a credit card.

"How about you, young man?" asked the hotel clerk. "Jeep holds six. Got plenty of room."

"Oh, I don't know—" Kozol began.

Virginia turned and smiled at him. "What's wrong?" she asked. "Have I scared you off Jeeps entirely?"

Tony laughed. "Don't be silly," he replied, though there may have been some element of the truth in her statement. "I-I didn't bring my wallet, that's all."

"Charge his fare to my card," she told the

clerk. To Tony she said, ''You can pay me back later.''

Kozol agreed. These Jeeps had doors, didn't they?

THEY HAD DOORS. But no windows.

Tony huddled in the back with the three strangers. Two guys and a girl who said they were college students from Los Angeles. The girl held hands with the sun-bleached blonde boy who looked like he could pose for a tanning oil ad.

Virginia sat up front next to their guide and driver, a young man named Brian, who drove the bright orange vehicle competently, if too quickly and fiercely through the winding, uneven dirt roads.

Brian wore a yellow buckskin jacket. His ponytail flopped like a kite tail in the wind. And the wind was bitter cold. It was like crossing through a wind tunnel. Only the windshield provided any protection at all, and only Virginia and Brian benefitted from that. The young couple cuddled. Tony and the other young man were forced to brave it alone.

They'd made several stops so far, to take in views of Cathedral Rock, Coffee Pot, The Nuns, Chimney Rock. The locals seemed to have a name for everything. Tony was beginning to think that if he picked up a pebble, he'd be able to turn it over and find its name chiseled on the underside. Like Bob, for instance.

Brian carefully explained the geologic history of the region and described the plant and wildlife dutifully and diligently. Answering basic questions he'd probably encountered hundreds of times before.

"Red is a color of power," explained their guide, as he led his small group through a path of cacti and yuccas. "According to some studies, people react more quickly, yet less efficiently under red light. It can also affect the electrical patterns of our bodies. Red places seem warmer, for instance."

That's funny, thought Kozol, as he hugged himself, they were surrounded by red rock and he was freezing his behind off.

"Ouch!" cried the young girl whose name Tony couldn't remember. She stopped and gingerly pulled some sort of cactus from her ankle.

Brian turned and said stoically, "Prickly pear are good at defining their territory."

Tony decided to pay closer attention to his footing.

"Any dangerous animals out here?" asked Virginia.

"Plenty of wildlife—" Brian stopped his march

now. The trail ended in a precipitous drop. "That's Oak Creek below, by the way. This area is home to the red-tailed hawk, several types of jays, muledeer, rabbit, squirrels, skunks. More than you would imagine. Most people think this is desert and devoid of life. When really it's the opposite. The environment here supports a great number of species, plant and animal."

"But dangerous animals?" asked the blonde boy.

Brian shrugged. "Black-tailed rattlesnakes, coyotes, even mountain lions—cougars."

Tony looked at his feet. No snakes. But what about beasts lurking in the bushes?

"The big cats are primarily nocturnal," spoke the guide, as if reading Tony's thoughts.

"I was reading in my guidebook about medicine wheels," Virginia said. "Are there any near here?"

"No, it's not part of this tour normally. But there is one not too distant, if you all wanted to see it?"

The young woman said, "What exactly is a medicine wheel?"

"Medicine wheels are constructed near centers of power. People build them out of stones. They are places of worship and spiritual healing." He said to the girl, "Would you like to see one?"

She nodded her head and everyone else agreed so they headed back to the Jeep.

Twenty treacherous minutes later Brian parked the vehicle high atop a ridge, one of the most prominent in the region. A filthy blue sedan was the only other vehicle in sight. Not exactly a major tourist attraction, Tony surmised.

"From here we will walk," he explained. "This mountain is quite sacred. A local woman bought this land many years ago to prevent developers from spoiling it. Greedy contractors from out of state were trying to buy up all the land to build a resort down there," he said, waving to the pristine valley below. "Now all you see is private land. And as I said, sacred land. Out of respect," Brian said solemnly, "I suggest that none of us speak from this point onward."

Everyone nodded earnestly and followed the strange guide through the melting snow and ankle sucking red mud as he led them around the top of the mountain. At one point Brian paused and whispered, "There," he said, pointing a thin finger, "at the juncture of those distant mountains, is the center of the universe. The birthplace of Everything."

Dutifully, the group paused and reflected upon this profound statement.

"You okay?" Tony whispered to Virginia,

who squatted atop a long flat rock. She nodded. Her face was nearly as red now as her hair.

After several minutes of inactivity during which Kozol feared he'd freeze some useful nether part off, their guide silently began walking briskly onward and the group hurried to follow as he disappeared down a narrow break between two Douglas fir trees.

Tony was glad to be moving. It warmed him—somewhat. The frigid air was barely cooled by his nostrils and came out in thin, puffy white clouds. As a kid, Tony used to enjoy the game of "blowing smoke." Now, his condensed breath only reminded him of how damn cold he was! He wished he were back in his room. Better yet back in Florida where his girlfriend, Nina Lasher, waited for him. A warm bed, a good... Tony stopped mid-stride.

Had he heard something? A rustling? His mind turned to thoughts of mountain lions and rattlesnakes. Vicious fangs and toxic venom. Did Guide Brian carry an emergency medical kit? Anti-venom?

Kozol turned around expecting to see Virginia who had been straggling behind. She was gone...

Then he heard a cry, distant but distinct.

"Help!"

Tony rushed back across the sharp rocky ledge

on the west side they had recently passed. Virginia had been walking perilously close to the cliff edge. She must have slipped! Kozol reached the edge and called, "Virginia?"

"Here!"

Tony leaned clumsily forward. After all, his feet, protected only by sneakers, were near frozen and virtually lifeless. He lost his balance and slid slowly back on the cold, wet ground. He groaned and struggled to his knees.

"Tony?"

"Yeah, I'm here. Just a sec—" He crawled to the precipice. Virginia stood on a tiny jut of rock below, dirty and scared. "Grab on!"

Virginia nodded and took Tony's hands.

Tony felt someone or something grabbing his calves from behind and braved a look. It was Brian holding him down. The others stood nearby offering support. With agonizing slowness, Virginia managed to climb over Kozol and top the ridge. Her breath came out short and hard.

"Thanks." The word came out like a two syllable sob.

Tony nodded and rolled over. The sun was high, and bright enough to hurt his eyes, but the cold, thin air had taken his breath away as well. He imagined it was like life on Neptune. Tony Kozol was sitting in what felt like thirty-five degree mud and didn't care. It could have been cougar dung and it wouldn't have mattered then.

"Can you walk?" Brian asked. He held out a gloved hand.

"Yes," Virginia said, rising uneasily. "Nothing's broken."

"The Gods are watching out for you." He patted Virginia's head. "The medicine wheel isn't far. We must give thanks."

Virginia nodded. "Thanks again, Tony," she whispered. "I thought we were going to die back there." She offered him a hand but Kozol managed to rise on his own.

"We?" Tony said. "You were in more danger than me."

"No, I meant—" Virginia abruptly stopped.

"Meant what?"

"Nothing." She leaned over and gave Tony a kiss.

Tony trembled. Her lips felt cold and warm at the same time.

Virginia looked round the tiny clearing. "We'd better catch up to the others." She looked towards the trees. Tony thought she seemed a bit uneasy. "I can't wait to see the medicine wheel."

Tony nodded. He hoped the medicine wheel had a real pharmacy. He could use an aspirin.

THE MEDICINE WHEEL was comprised of a circle of rocks maybe fifty feet in diameter with a break at the near end. A smaller ring of rocks, which Kozol estimated to be about thirty feet in diameter came next, with four spokes, each representing the four directions, according to Brian, leading to a smaller circle of rocks in the center. This circle was only about six feet across.

Brian kneeled outside the first ring of rocks and opened his jacket to remove a plastic baggy from which he extracted something that appeared to be dried plant material. Pot?

Tony looked questioningly at Virginia.

"I think it's sage," she whispered in his ear.

The group looked on as Brian removed a lighter from his pocket and carefully ignited the plant as it lay on the flat rock before him. He said a prayer which Tony didn't understand.

Brian gestured to Virginia first. "Take some of this," he said, pulling another plastic pouch from within his chest pocket. "It's tobacco, a gift for the Gods. Do as I do. The Wheel is Life. Our Spirits are like the Wind circling ever round."

Brian said another prayer then entered the circle. He moved counterclockwise, stopping to throw bits of tobacco every few steps. Virginia mimicked the guide, as did the others, including Tony. Though he felt sheepish doing so.

Slowly, the group made its way around the wheel. Brian went to the small circle in the center and said a prayer. Everyone else remained silent. They stood that way for many minutes. Tony watched as Brian raised his hands to the clear blue sky. In supplication, he supposed. Then the odd guide nodded to Virginia and the others and they returned to the Jeep in silence.

The only noise as they drove down the mountain was the hum of the Jeep's tires over the mud and rock, comingled with the ringing of the cold wind. The only smell the scent of burning oil, the strain of its overheating engine.

Tony lay as low as possible. His new clothes were soiled and damp. Useless. Virginia seemed to have fallen asleep up front. While the college kids were equally quiet.

BRIAN GENTLY SHOOK Virginia's shoulder. "Home at last," he said, shoving the gear shift into neutral.

The Red Rock Resort never looked so good to Tony. The calming scent of smouldering eucalyptus escaped lazily from the lobby's stone chimney. Kozol hopped out the back of the vehicle. Virginia winced as he helped her down as well.

"Ouch!" she cried.

"You all right?" Tony asked.

"Yeah, my right leg's a little sore, that's all."
She hobbled tentatively towards the main lobby.
"Must have stiffened up from sitting. Hey," she
said with a start, "isn't that your car?"

Tony followed her gaze. His rented Chevy occupied a spot near the restaurant up front. "Looks
like it, all right. I called the rental company to
complain when I arrived and I guess I'd forgotten
all about it after that." The flat had been repaired.

A doorman approached. "Your car?"

Tony nodded his head.

"They towed it up after lunch. Key's inside at
the desk." The doorman held the door open for
Virginia and Kozol.

"Hold on while I get the key to the Chevy and
I'll drive you down to your room, Virginia."

"Don't bother, I can walk."

Tony grabbed her arm. "Don't be silly. You're
limping like an old maid. It's gotta be a quarter
mile down the hill. I'll drive you. Wait here."
Kozol pushed her into the nearest chair and faced
his nemesis, Mark, the assistant manager and
chief jerk.

"Funny," began Mark, "I wasn't aware of any
mud baths in the region. Though I'm certain the
red earth could be quite restorative." He stuck the
key to the Chevy on the counter, in anticipation
of Tony's request.

Kozol took the key. "Thanks. And yes, the mud is quite refreshing. I only hope you get a chance to try it yourself. Soon."

"If I do," Mark replied with a smile, "I believe I shall remove my outer garments first."

Tony turned his back and took a step.

"Oh, Mr. Kozol—"

"Yes?"

"Your suitcase arrived while you were out. I had it sent down to your room for you."

Tony hated what he was about to say. "Thank you, Mark."

KOZOL FOUND A SPOT for the Chevy in front of Virginia's building and walked the girl to her door. Virginia unlocked it and Tony looked inside. "Wow," he said. "That's weird."

"You mean the jacuzzi in the middle of the room? Doesn't everybody have one?"

Tony shook his head. "Not me." The large tub stood on a raised pink tiled stand against the wall opposite the king-sized bed. A variety of colored bath salts and bubble solutions lined the back edge. "It's like a shrine or a bizarre ritualistic altar of some sort."

"It's unusual, alright. Especially since there's an ordinary tub in the bathroom as well. But I love bubble baths and this jacuzzi is a great place for one. You can even see the t.v. from here.''

"Well, just don't slip and fall again. I don't know if I can handle another rescue. Though," he said with a wolfish grin, "if I had to perform a rescue, saving a naked girl from a warm jacuzzi would be a lot more—" he paused, "interesting, than plucking a clothed one off the side of a cliff.''

"Don't worry," answered Virginia. "You won't have to rescue me. I'm not the slip and fall type.''

"Could've fooled me.''

"You mean back there?" Virginia shrugged. "Oh, I didn't slip.''

Kozol raised his eyebrows.

"I was pushed.''

Virginia gently pushed the door shut in Tony's startled face.

SIX

"WHERE HAVE YOU BEEN?"

Tony shut his eyes and opened them again.

Regretfully, Det. Gibson was still standing there, leaning awkwardly against a wooden post near the entrance of the conference exhibit hall. Wearing a black suit that made her look even more manly than the brown one had before. She looked even less like she belonged at a New Age conference than Kozol did himself.

"Taking a Jeep tour," he said in answer to her question. "Came back, cleaned up and thought I'd come check out the exhibits and sit in on some of the lectures this afternoon. Problem?"

Det. Gibson squeezed her lips tightly together. Tony noticed they were cracked and dried. The effects of an arid environment, no doubt. He wondered if she ever thought of applying lipstick.

"No more than I had this morning. Found your prints on a glass in your friend's room."

"So we had a drink together. Talked about old times."

"What did you drink?"

"Scotch. Why? You must've seen the bottle."

Gibson shook her head no. "We didn't find any bottle in the room."

"So? You think a bottle of scotch could be important?"

"Probably not, but I don't like things that aren't there."

Tony let this unusual concept sink in. "You think I took it?"

"Already searched your room."

"Of course."

The detective made no response.

"Well, if that's all—" Tony turned away.

Det. Gibson grabbed his sleeve. "Your friend, Janvilhelm Rein Wunderkind, his driver's license reads John Vincent Ryan."

Tony shrugged. "I know that. So the guy changed his name? Janvilhelm sounds a lot better to people like these than John Ryan. Don't you think?"

"I suppose," admitted the detective. "All I really want to know is who killed him and why. Aren't you curious?"

"You so sure it was murder?" Kozol asked in low tones.

Det. Gibson said yes. "Coroner's pretty sure. The type of injury, the angle of the body—"

"Jesus…"

"Amen," said Gibson. "So," she asked, fold-

ing her arms stiffly across her fairly ample chest,
"who?"

"Who what?"

Det. Gibson looked around the room. "Who
did it?"

Kozol looked confused. The hall was filled with
interested browsers. A couple dozen tables were
set up in uneven rows with people selling crystals,
offering auric readings, tarot, palmistry, aura photos, massage, spiritual healing, chakra balancing,
lots of books. There was even a table set up hawk-
ing Janvilhelm's music on CD and cassette. There
was a big crowd around that table. The biggest.

Death sells, Tony thought, as he watched the
ghoulish spectacle. Janvilhelm would probably
sell more music in the coming months than ever
before. "Finding that out is your job."

"Let's play a game," began Gibson. "Let's as-
sume that someone here did it. Oh, maybe not
somebody in this room, but at this conference."
She softened her look and asked again, "Who did
it?"

Tony was stumped. "I have no idea. There are
two or three hundred people at this conference. I
can't even imagine why!"

"You were his friend. You must know something."

"I'd barely seen or spoken to John in years.

Surely, there must be others here who knew him better. John told me that many of them often worked together. Like Dr. Owen, Annie Campbell, and Suzette—''

"Miss Aristotle?" Det. Gibson rubbed her nose. "She's got a made up name, too, it turns out."

"I'm not surprised."

"She's giving me nothing but grief all day about those stupid skulls of hers. It's the first time I've ever found myself trying to hide from a crime victim!"

"So they never turned up?"

"No. Could be they're long gone by now. After all, everybody here would recognize them. According to Miss Aristotle, they are nearly priceless. Did Janvilhelm ever mention them to you, Kozol?"

"No. Why do you ask that?"

"He's dead and the crystal skulls are missing. All in one night." She raised a finger. "One crushed skull and two stolen ones. You like coincidences, Kozol?" Det. Gibson didn't wait to hear his answer. "I don't." She turned on her low black heels and departed.

Tony felt a stab in his back and turned. It was Annie Campbell.

"Woman's a bit stiff, don't you think? Living

in a town like Sedona, one would expect the sheriff to be a bit more—'' Miss Campbell paused. ''Laid back maybe?''

''I don't believe she's a sheriff.''

''Whatever. The woman is casting a terrible, dark aura over the entire conference. It's bad enough that Maggie and Azul are missing.''

''Yeah, Miss Aristotle was quite upset when I saw her this morning.''

Annie Campbell pulled Tony over to a couple of free chairs along the near wall. ''Yes, can you imagine? Maggie and Azul are famous. Without them, Suzette has nothing.''

''Then why steal them?''

Miss Campbell rested a hand on Tony's knee. ''For the power,'' she whispered.

''Power?''

''Yes, the power of the Ramadians. Don't you see?''

Tony said he didn't.

''Whoever possesses the crystal skulls may have discovered a way of unlocking their hidden knowledge. With that power they can control the world!''

Kozol tried real hard not to laugh. So he simply grinned. ''I don't know. It seems so farfetched, Annie.''

"It could be Dr. Owen," she suggested, "or Ralph Bernes."

"Who's that?"

"The psychic from England. Surely you've heard of him?"

"No. Is he here at the conference?"

"Yes, of course. He gave a lecture this morning. It was wonderful, I might add. That's him at the big booth in the corner giving readings."

"I'm afraid I missed it," Tony replied. Following Annie's gaze, he saw Ralph Bernes seated at a low, black draped table with, of all things, a crystal ball atop it. Even seated, Kozol could see that Ralph Bernes was a large man. He had jet black hair combed back atop his pear-shaped head and a full beard to match. He wore a black suit with a cape. Another odd bird.

Miss Campbell shrugged and went on. "I'm afraid I'm a bit—" she looked round the hall, "—disenchanted with Ralph Bernes, myself, this morning."

"Why is that?" Kozol asked. He felt himself getting sucked deeper and deeper into a conversation which he cared nothing about and saw no point to pursuing. Surely someone would come and rescue him soon, but who?

Annie leaned closer. "Well, I suppose it isn't

my place to say it, but Mr. Bernes seems awfully fond of Camille.''

"Camille?"

"You know," Miss Campbell said under her breath, "Dr. Owen Kennedy's pretty young wife.''

"Are you implying that they—''

Annie nodded. "I saw them in the outdoor jacuzzi down by the pool last night. Cuddling. Very, very cozily, if you know what I mean,'' said Miss Campbell coyly. "Naked.''

"About what time was this?" He turned his attention as he spoke back to Ralph Bernes, who suddenly had become far more interesting a character.

"Late. Very late. One or two in the morning, I'd say.''

Tony looked at Miss Campbell and said, "That's awfully late to be out and about. Do you mind if I ask what you were doing?''

Annie smiled. "Communicating, of course. The sky was clear, the stars' presence sharp and pulsating. Energy swirling down and entering me—''

Tony squirmed uneasily. Was the woman getting aroused? "I think I get the idea." It was a lie, but he knew she'd believe it.

She did.

"I knew you would understand," Annie said.

She patted his hand and kissed his cheek. "I must go. I'm giving a talk soon in Mystic Hall. The police have opened it back up."

"Already?"

"Yes, though they've removed the piano for evidence. Can you imagine?"

"They'll probably check it for fingerprints."

"Yes, I hadn't thought of that," said Annie after a moment. "So, can I count on seeing you there, Tony?"

"Huh?"

"At my lecture, silly."

Like a deer trapped in the headlights, Kozol agreed. He hoped she was going to take a cold shower first. Tony could have used one about then himself. What he knew was that Annie Campbell had as much a reason for wanting the crystal skulls as anyone. After all, she claimed to communicate with the Ramadians. Perhaps she wanted them all to herself...

As for Camille Kennedy, where was she at the time that Janvilhelm was being killed? Perhaps he should ask the psychic, Ralph Bernes. Extraperceptual abilities or not, the man might have some answers.

Kozol slowly rose and wandered over towards Ralph Bernes' Psychic Powers booth. A drastically overweight woman draped in a purple dress was holding Ralph's hands in her own. As large a man as he was, the woman's hands engulfed his like a couple of catcher's mitts.

"Thank you for coming," said the psychic, rising and helping the woman rise as well.

She thanked him effusively and turned to Tony. She wiped a tear from one puffy brown eye. She said to Tony with a smile, "He's such a dear, wonderful man," and shuffled off.

Tony smiled back silently. What could he say?

"Come in, young man," came Ralph Bernes' deep baritone voice. He gave a theatrical sweep of his cape and stepped aside for Tony to enter the large booth which was closed off by low curtained walls. "Have a seat." Bernes gestured towards the newly vacated chair.

Tony sat.

Bernes deposited himself across the little table and laid his hands on either side of the crystal ball. "I know you."

"You do?"

"Of course," replied Ralph Bernes. "You were at the concert last night—with Janvilhelm."

"That's right. In fact, I wanted to—"

Bernes cut him off with the wave of his hand and a soothing word. Tony noticed a gold band on his ring finger. Married? "Don't say another word. I understand. You are troubled, Mr. Kozol.

The world has struck you a great blow. The future
is uncertain." He waved his arms over the crystal
ball.

For a moment, Tony wondered if the room was
getting darker. Had somebody dimmed the lights
or was it an illusion which Bernes had planted in
his mind?

"You seek answers."

"Yes, but…"

"I can help you. Relax…close your eyes, Mr.
Kozol."

"If I could just—"

Quietly Ralph Bernes repeated, "Close your
eyes, Mr. Kozol…"

Tony reluctantly shut his eyes. After the last
couple of days he could've used a quick forty
winks. Bernes' words rambled on in mesmerizing
tones. The man was good.

"Your friend has been murdered. I see it
clearly."

"You do?" Tony blinked and opened his eyes.

"Uh-uh." Bernes pushed Kozol's eyelids down
with his cool fingers. "Eyes closed, please. It
helps me to concentrate…to see what is inside
your mind…your soul…" The psychic sighed.
"Yes, I see. You seek answers. Janvilhelm's
death disturbs your soul."

"Yes. Can you tell me who killed him?"

Maybe Bernes would confess to the murder himself so they could stop this charade.

"No," answered the psychic, sadly. "Yet, perhaps Janvilhelm can— If we can summon his spirit to us…"

"That would be great," said Tony. "If you do reach him, tell him he forgot to sign my paycheck."

"Please, Mr. Kozol," shot Bernes sternly, "it is utmost important that we do not mock the spirits. If we do not believe, they shall not come to us."

"Sorry."

Ralph Bernes cleared his throat and said, "I shall attempt a manifestation. Please concentrate, Mr. Kozol."

Tony held his eyes shut and all he could picture was Janvilhelm stuck in that grand piano in Mystic Hall.

Bernes emitted a low moan. It sounded like a bass foghorn. Then he spoke. "Janvilhelm Rein Wunderkind. He is here. Janvilhelm wishes you well, Tony."

Tony whispered, "Who killed you, John?"

"I'm sorry," replied the psychic. "Janvilhelm cannot or will not help us. I feel his presence in my mind like waves of music on the spiritual shore. Janvilhelm is troubled but cannot be of mortal help. We must—'' Bernes paused and wiped his brow, "look for the light, ourselves." The psychic exhaled like he was blowing out the candles on a birthday cake.

Tony opened his eyes. "That's it?"

Bernes said with a shrug, "The spirits do not always cooperate."

"Mmm," Tony replied. "I bet you get more cooperation from mortals."

"How do you mean?" The psychic sounded quickly defensive.

"Like Camille Kennedy, for instance. I hear she's pretty—" Tony smiled, "cooperative."

Ralph Bernes pushed his chair back from the reading table. "I'm afraid I don't know what you are talking about, Mr. Kozol. And," he added, "our time is up."

"One moment," Tony hurried on. "You were naked out in the hot tub with Camille doing the wild thing in the middle of the night. That's about the same time that Janvilhelm was murdered. Maybe you or Camille know something about it...? Maybe the two of you killed him yourselves?"

"You are quite mistaken," Bernes answered. "Your facts are incorrect and if you continue with such slander my attorneys will tear you to ribbons."

Kozol said, "Maybe. Then again, maybe the police would like to talk to you about it. Maybe," he said, rising and leaning over the table towards the big man, "they'd like to speak with Mrs. Camille Kennedy about it."

The psychic frowned and pulled his beard. "Camille and I were having a psychic consultation, Mr. Kozol. Nothing more."

Tony sneered.

"The water, the atmosphere…" Bernes went on, "…these things can be very conducive to conducting a successful psychic reading."

"Ah," Tony said. "The personal touch."

"Exactly."

"You know," said Kozol. "Janvilhelm may not have been the most perfect person in the world, but he didn't deserve to die like that."

Ralph Bernes folded his hands. "I never suggested he did."

"Were you and Camille Kennedy together the whole time?"

"We were."

"She didn't run off for a little while, maybe to drop a piano on Janvilhelm's head?"

The big man was unmoving.

Tony sighed. "How long were the two of you—" he wanted to say screwing but decided upon, "engaged?"

The psychic grinned wickedly. "I'm afraid I wasn't wearing my watch."

Kozol tried to shut out the beastly image of Ralph Bernes naked in a hot tub with a young beauty like Camille Kennedy. What did she see in the guy? For that matter, what did she see in her husband? "So long, Bernes. If I were you, I'd lay off the midnight jacuzzis."

"One moment, Mr. Kozol."

"Yes?"

Ralph Bernes pointed to a large orange sign with blue lettering which hung over the billowy white drape along the back of the booth. Upon it, a fee schedule was clearly posted. "That'll be fifty dollars for the session," he said churlishly.

Tony looked at the sign and groaned. Fifty dollars? Then he smiled and tapped his forehead. "I'm thinking of my address," he said. "Bill me."

Kozol turned and walked away. Even though he was no New Age Spiritualist and laid claim to no special mental powers, he could feel the irate psychic's eye balls burning wide holes in the back of his head.

Tony quickened his steps.

SEVEN

"THERE YOU ARE."

Dr. Kennedy stood blocking the entrance to Mystic Hall. "I've been looking for you everywhere, Mr. Kozol."

Tony took a step backward. Had Owen Kennedy heard about his conversation with Ralph Bernes already? Was he about to take a swing at him? "Dr. Kennedy—" Kozol braced himself. "Looking for me? What for?"

Dr. Kennedy laid his hand on Tony's shoulder. "I need to ask you a big favor, son."

Tony tried to slouch away but the doctor held him. "Sure, anything."

Owen smiled. "Terrific. I knew I could count on you." He squeezed Tony's neck.

"Absolutely."

"Going in to see Miss Campbell?"

"Yes, I told her I would attend her lecture."

Dr. Kennedy nodded his approval. "I'm certain you won't be disappointed."

That's funny, thought Kozol, because he was pretty certain he would. "Right, well, I'd better get a seat—"

Owen Kennedy ignored his cue and said, "Terrible, just terrible about Janvilhelm. The man was like a son to me, you know."

Tony asked, "How long did the two of you know one another?"

"Oh," said Dr. Kennedy, waving his free hand through the air, "many, many lifetimes. Many transformations."

"What about your wife, Camille? Was she fond of Janvilhelm also?"

"Oh, exceedingly so," replied the doctor. "My wife loves everyone."

Tony wondered just how much the good doctor knew about his wife's love. "I can't imagine who would want him dead—" It was a leading question, but Owen seemed to ignore the bait.

"Nor I," he stated. "Now, about that favor—"

"Yes?"

"The main concert is scheduled for nine this evening, after dinner. Here, in Mystic Hall. As you can see, the Sedona police have graciously allowed us reentry."

"So I heard."

"I don't know what we would have done had they not. Then again, we don't have to worry about that now, do we?"

Tony agreed.

Dr. Kennedy patted Kozol on the back. "Do the best you can."

"Sure," said Tony. He took half a step then stopped. "Wait."

"Yes?" said the doctor.

"Do the best I can what?"

"Why play, of course."

"Play?! You mean you want me to get up there and give a concert by myself?" A cold sweat seemed to wash over Kozol like a coat of doom.

"Yes, precisely, Tony. The show must go on and all that." Dr. Kennedy clutched Kozol's arm. "It's what Janvilhelm would have wanted."

"I don't know—"

"Everyone would be so disappointed. In fact," said Owen Kennedy, smiling brightly, "we can call it a tribute to Janvilhelm Rein Wunderkind!" He grinned like a two hundred watt light bulb. "I'll go make a special announcement right now."

"Owen wait! I can't possibly give an entire concert." Tony pleaded in desperation. "Can't you find someone else?"

Dr. Kennedy shook his head. "You'll do fine. I sense an aura about you."

"I hate to shatter your illusions, but that's fear you're smelling, doctor!"

Owen Kennedy laughed. "Trust me. Besides," he added, "I can pay you an extra two thousand."

Tony's mouth stopped just long enough for his need of cash to overtake his fear of performing a bunch of music that he didn't know. Two thousand dollars. "Okay," he gulped.

"Wonderful. Oh, and about my wife, Camille," Dr. Kennedy said by way of caution, "don't let what you might hear fool you. We are very much in love."

Tony said nothing.

"I know that Camille has a special way of showing, should I say, sharing, her love with others. Men and women alike. It's why I adore her, I suppose." The doctor's bottomless eyes gazed upon Kozol. "I wouldn't want Camille disturbed in any way. I wouldn't want anything unpleasant said of her. Do you understand?"

Tony understood. Two thousand dollars worth.

Kozol cringed as the doctor rose to the podium to introduce Annie Campbell's lecture on the Wisdom of the Ramadians. Before introducing her, as promised, Owen Kennedy announced the Janvilhelm Rein Wunderkind Memorial Concert to take place that evening in Mystic Hall. The crowd applauded heartily. Kozol shut his eyes and tried to find a way out— Preferably a way that let him keep the money.

Annie Campbell began speaking of her early years, of her first discovering that the Ancient Race, the Ramadians, had chosen her to be their contact on Earth, their vessel for the fountain of knowledge…he felt the words falling like stones upon his head…thunk-thunk-thunk…and he fell asleep.

TONY'S HEAD popped back with a start. As his eyes sought focus he saw that people were slowly filing out of the lecture room. A bunch more were gathered around the table where Annie Campbell had sat giving her electrifying lecture. He walked over.

She smiled. "How did you find my story, Tony?"

"I found it—" he sought the right word, "riveting." After all, he hadn't moved for an hour and a half. And he finally felt rested. Maybe rested enough to give a halfway decent performance.

"Would you care to join me for a walk before dinner? I find the red earth quite stimulating."

"No, thanks," Kozol replied. "Too cold for me. I was looking for Suzette. Have you seen her?" He was hoping to hear Miss Aristotle's theories concerning the stolen crystal skulls.

"I'm afraid not, Tony. Try her room."

Tony said he would and with that in mind he

asked the girl at reception for Miss Aristotle's room number. Thankfully, Mark was nowhere in sight. There was no answer at Suzette's room.

Kozol wandered back over to the exhibit hall. Ralph Bernes was speaking softly to Chief Howling Wind, who was now garbed in more traditional western attire, whereas earlier and the day previous, the Chief had appeared in more typical American Indian dress. He still had a feather headdress atop his head, however, bearing a single feather that looked to be eagle. Incongruous as it was with the polo shirt and khakis he wore now.

Kozol walked up to the nearest booth, a couple offering video taped aura readings, whatever that was and asked, "Excuse me, have either of you seen Miss Aristotle lately?"

"Sorry," said the young man. "It's been crazy around here. This is the first moment of rest we've had. Boy, could I use a massage." The woman he was working with dutifully began rubbing the small of his back.

"Care for a reading?" asked the slender girl.

"No, thanks," Tony answered. "I'm trying to cut down."

The young woman nodded as if she understood. Funny, Kozol was beginning to understand just how easy it was to get by in a place like this.

People understood him even when there was no meaning to his words.

Now that was heavy.

Tony thanked them once again. It was time for some fresh air and a change of pace. He got in his car and headed up towards the city of Sedona proper.

Several miles up, near the junction of Highways 89A and 179, he came to a stop. It was up near the spot where he and Virginia had first come when they had overshot the Red Rock Resort. A mixed shopping and arts and crafts village called Tlaquepaque occupied the entire left corner. It looked like as good a place as any to get out and stretch his legs. Kozol turned in and parked.

He pulled up his collar. The sun was sinking behind the high hills and cold seeped up from the ground like an invisible sludge.

Located on the bank of Oak Creek, Tlaquepaque was a unique and intriguing center of restaurants, art studios, jewelers, clothing and trinkets. Mostly of western motif. Like just about everything in Sedona seemed to be. This was not a place where one was likely to find French Provincial furniture or Scandinavian design bookshelves. A whiff of fresh baked bread tweaked his appetite.

Tlaquepaque had been the inspired dream of a

Nevada entrepreneur who, in the early 1970's decided to build the complex as a dedicated arts center. It had been modeled on the artisans' village of San Pedro Tlaquepaque, near Guadalajara, Mexico. Commanding sycamores writhed through the tiled walkways and around the quiet court yards, as if the buildings had sprung up around them. There were numerous such interior courtyards, each unique, nestled between the hacienda-like buildings and quaint, cobblestoned roads.

Tlaquepaque had been a failure of sorts at first. The initial idea had been that artists and crafts people would have their galleries on the ground floor and live upstairs. It wasn't until it was decided to further commercialize the area by leasing out shop space on the second floors and bringing in stores and eateries of a somewhat broader nature, that the failing center was revitalized.

Now, Tlaquepaque was a tourist attraction in and of itself. A must see for those who passed through the red rock country of Sedona. And Kozol himself had fallen prey to its lure.

Tony wandered through the shops, wincing at prices as he went. Was it that expensive or was he that poor? He came to the gloomy conclusion that it was a little of both.

Kozol stopped outside a restaurant window. A flash of red hair had caught his eye. Standing alone at the crowded bar was Virginia Garner, looking out of place in jeans and a heavy down jacket, while most the restaurant's patrons wore elegant evening attire. He went around the side and entered.

Tony nodded to the hostess and told her he was meeting someone at the bar. She looked at him dubiously but let him pass.

"Hi," said Virginia sullenly. She set her wine glass atop the black bar and waved to the bartender for another.

Tony noted a slight slur in her voice. "Are you sure you want more?"

Virginia gave him an icy stare. Tony shuffled his feet. "You my father or something?"

"Sorry," said Kozol. "I was only trying to help."

The redhead lifted her glass, took a sip and set the glass carefully back down. She rubbed her belly. "Nothing can help. Not now."

"Then why drink?"

"Why not?"

The barkeep asked Tony for his order. He asked for a glass of light beer. Kozol handed over a five dollar bill expecting some change but all he got was a dirty look. "Listen, Virginia," he said awkwardly, "I don't know what's bothering you, but if you want to talk about it—"

Virginia Garner gave him another of her patented icy stares. "No thanks, Tony. Besides, if you're smart, you'll get out of here. Out of Sedona…out of the New Age." She laughed.

"I'd like some answers first."

"What are the questions?"

He swallowed a mouthful of beer and went on. "Like who killed Janvilhelm?"

Virginia's face metamorphosed from sullen to angry. Her voice rose. "John, call the fool John. That was his name…not Janvilhelm!"

All eyes looked their way. "Sorry," whispered Kozol.

Virginia sighed. "Yeah." She stared for a moment at her reflection in the mirror behind the bar. "You know John killed himself."

"That's not what Detective Gibson says."

"Oh, somebody might have dropped a piano on his skull, but he put himself there."

Tony thought about this for a moment. These New Agers could be tricky. "You mean he was responsible for his own death?"

"Aren't we all?" An empty glass stood forlornly before her. Tony wondered how many glasses she'd had before he arrived.

"Det. Gibson thinks it might have something to do with the crystal skulls."

"Maggie and Azul belong to the people of

Mexico. That bitch, Suzette stole them from the people! The ancient skulls are part of their heritage…'' Virginia beamed, a twinkle in her red eyes.

Green eyes and red capillaries. Gazing into Miss Garner's otherwise luscious eyes was like gazing at a Christmas scene. All that was missing now was the image of the manger in her pupils.

''With luck, they shall be returned to the people of Mexico.''

''You took them?''

Virginia leaned forward. Her breath smelled of alcohol and the little, salted peanuts she had been nibbling on. ''The thought crossed my mind. It's why I came here…''

''But you can't steal something like that—'' Tony glanced nervously about the room. The last thing he needed was to get arrested as a co-conspirator in the theft of two ridiculous skulls named Maggie and Azul. ''You've got to turn yourself in—''

''Relax, Kozol. I haven't got them.''

''Then who does?''

It was Virginia's turn to shrug. She paused and called the bartender.

''No,'' said Tony, putting a hand over her glass. ''You've had enough.''

''Yes, Daddy.''

"Very funny." He grabbed her by the shoulders, gently. "You didn't answer my question. Who's got Maggie and Azul?"

Virginia looked amused. "I honestly don't know. They were stolen before I'd even had a chance to try."

"Then what makes you think the crystal skulls may be returned to Mexico?"

"I've been dropping some hints…letting comments slip…making my opinion known. By now, everyone involved in the conference should know that I'd like to see Maggie and Azul returned to the Yucatan. Maybe whoever took the skulls will contact me."

"Or maybe it's all a smokescreen and you've got the skulls yourself. Mind if I search your room?"

"Yes, I do. Besides, I'm sure the police have searched all our rooms by now. The skulls aren't there."

"I noticed you speaking to Janvilhelm last night after the concert…before he died. Did he mention the skulls to you?"

"No."

"You looked like you were having an argument—"

Virginia tossed Tony's comment off. "He

made some lewd remark and I put him in his place.''

Kozol nodded. That sounded like his old college roommate.

"You gonna finish that?''

"No," replied Tony, pushing his beer glass out of her reach, "and neither are you.''

She scowled.

"I've got to hit the men's room. When I get back, I'll give you a ride back to the resort.''

"I've got my own car—''

"Forget it. You're in no condition to be driving anywhere. I'll be right back.'' Tony pushed his way through the crowd. When he returned, Virginia was nowhere in sight. The bathroom? No, he should have passed her. "Excuse me," he said to the barkeeper, "but did you see where the redhead I was speaking to went?''

The man grinned. "Finished your beer and walked out.'' He wiped a ring of moisture from the counter.

Tony ran out the door and looked in all directions. Virginia was gone.

EIGHT

"STOP!"

Suzette asked, "What's wrong, Tony?"

"Slow down. Up ahead. I see police lights. And that looks like Virginia Garner's Wrangler—"

Suzette silently pulled her car over to the shoulder. Three police cars blocked the oncoming lane. Half of a red Jeep with California plates jutted over the edge of the road, dangling helplessly in mid-air. Another car which Tony didn't recognize was squashed face-first like an accordion against a boulder on the opposite edge of the road, with its trunk popped open, probably from the impact of the crash.

An ambulance crew, with the assistance of local Fire Rescue were pulling a woman from the driver's side of the Jeep.

Tony recognized the parka and red hair immediately. "Virginia!" He bolted from the car and was held back by an officer.

"You know her?"

"Yeah, Virginia Garner. She's staying at the Red Rock Resort, like me. What's happened?"

The lean officer shrugged. "Anybody's guess.

But this one," he said jerking his thumb at Virginia as the paramedics lifted her into the back of the waiting ambulance, "is drunk as a skunk."

Tony nodded lamely. "I'd seen her drinking in town earlier. Then she disappeared."

"Where was this?"

"I don't know the name...that French place over in Tlaquepaque."

"Makes sense. Her car is headed in the right direction if she was going from there back to the hotel."

"Can I speak with her?"

"It's up to the paramedics."

Tony ran over to the ambulance and stuck his head in the rear. "She okay?"

"Not too bad," said the medic as he adjusted the straps to hold the girl down while they headed out to the medical center. "A lot better than the one that got pulled out of that Nissan."

"They tried to run me over." Virginia opened her eyes and focused on Tony. "They tried to run me over."

"Who did?" Tony asked.

"The other car."

"Is she really okay?" Tony inquired of the paramedic. He nodded. "Yeah, she keeps saying that. Trying to blame the other driver, if you ask me. I expect she's more drunk than anything.

She'll have a bigger headache from the booze than she will that accident. She was lucky. A lot luckier than that other lady.''

"The other driver was a woman?''

"That's right.'' He adjusted the last strap and said, "Gotta go now. Don't worry, your friend will be home as soon as the emergency department looks her over. I've seen worse than this go home.''

"What about the driver of the Nissan? Did she make it?''

He shrugged. "Who knows? They took her first. You see that car. That's gotta smart.''

Tony stepped back as the driver closed the rear doors and sped off into the darkness. A tow truck was hitching up the Nissan. "Bad, huh?'' Tony remarked.

"She hit real hard,'' replied the tow truck operator without so much as turning his head.

Kozol felt a tug at his sleeve.

"Come on, Tony,'' Suzette said softly. "There's nothing more you can do.''

Tony nodded and walked back to the car with Suzette's arm locked in his.

"That was a great concert you gave back there,'' Suzette said as she turned left at the "Y", as the junction of Highway 179 and Highway 89A was known locally. This was the dividing point between Uptown Sedona and West Sedona. Uptown Sedona is the principle tourist section of the city, whereas West Sedona is largely residential.

Suzette was heading out towards West Sedona. Tony knew that much from his Mystery Jeep Tour earlier that day. He rubbed the fingertips of his left hand. His fingers were stiff and his fingertips sore. Kozol hadn't played guitar that long, that hard since his college frat days with Janvilhelm and their loosely held together band.

In fact, if John and he hadn't been pushed by John's driven girlfriend and manager, Lindi Light, they probably never would have made any money at all. John liked to party at that time more than he liked to practice. John had been a child prodigy of sorts, playing four hours a day even as a young boy. When he'd finally gone off to college it was like a great release for him. Through talent alone he had survived himself. And now he was dead. Killed by a piano no less.

Tony said, "I'm just glad it's over." He followed the stars moving overhead as seen through Suzette's moonroof. "How far is this house of yours?"

"Not far." She patted Tony on the leg. "In a hurry?"

Tony squirmed. "No."

Suzette stared at the road and Tony stared at

the girl. She gave off a sexuality even driving a car. So she called herself Princess of Proxima Centauri and Keeper of the Crystal Skulls? Kozol figured he could easily ignore and overcome Miss Aristotle's quirky personality, as overridden as it was by her own heavenly body.

"That's City Hall and the police station." Suzette pointed to a low building on the right.

"Any news about Maggie and Azul?"

"No," answered Suzette sadly. "That detective said they were doing all they could. But they don't seem to care…"

"Well, they do have a murder to investigate."

"Maybe so, but Maggie and Azul are priceless."

"Virginia seems to think they ought to be returned to Mexico—"

Suzette laughed. "I purchased Maggie and Azul from the poor family that owned them. A family named Montero from a tiny village near Veracruz in Mexico. It was completely legal. The skulls had been in their possession for several generations or more. Can I help it if they were for sale?"

Tony nodded in sympathy.

"The money I gave the Monteros went for food and clothing and to the education of their five children. Besides, what would Miss Garner do?

Give everything back to whatever country it originally came from? To whatever government was in power? Think what that would do to the world museums.''

Kozol sighed. Suzette had a point. Perhaps Virginia had been overzealous. And saying that someone was out first to push her over a cliff and next to run her off the road, that was simply absurd. And finally, being three sheets to the wind hadn't helped Virginia's case.

They drove off on a dark strip of road. "I can't believe how brilliant the stars are out here," Tony remarked.

"No light pollution," explained Suzette. "There are almost no streetlights."

"That's right," said a surprised Tony. "I hadn't even realized it until you said it." There wasn't a streetlight in sight and he hadn't even seen any along Highway 179 where Virginia had crashed.

"It's got something to do with the Lowell Observatory up near Flagstaff. It's a working astronomic facility, you know. So the light pollution is kept to a minimum. It's the law."

They winded several times around a hill. A circular shaped house stood at the top, commanding a view of open valleys and dark mountains. The

few lights in the distance Tony took for home-
steads such as Suzette's.

"This is your house?" he said in awe. The
home was of sleek, modern design. And big. He
couldn't help wondering how much a place like
that had cost. More than he would ever likely af-
ford...

"Not really, but a friend lets me use it when
I'm in town."

"Some friend—"

Suzette unlocked the door from the garage to
the house. "Come on in." She flipped on a light
switch, exposing a tidy laundry room and side en-
try area. "Fix us a drink while I check on the cat
and get out of these heels. The bar is in the living
room off to the left."

Kozol said he'd find his way.

THEY MADE LOVE in a spacious bed in a room
surrounded on three sides by glass. A peeping tom
would have needed a high powered telescope to
get even a peek. Maybe the gang up at Lowell
Observatory were looking in.

Settled back on his pillow, Kozol cranked open
one tired eyelid and tried to imagine the observatory somewhere out there in the darkness. It
was hopeless. Tony had no idea what direction he

was looking in. Hell, he didn't even know where he was.

She ran a hand along the inside of his thigh and said, "More music?" He nodded. Suzette rose naked and shameless from the bed and changed the CD in the player. It was New Age music but at least it wasn't Janvilhelm Rein Wunderkind. "Be right back," she cooed.

Tony admired her shapely rear as she departed. She'd been wild, but nearly silent in bed. Kozol was exhausted. Two empty crystal goblets lie on the floor, beside a drained bottle of champagne.

Outside, stars lit the sky like silent fireworks. The room they occupied was decorated with modern touches, chrome and black, brilliantly polished wood. Abstract sculptures that reminded Kozol of dancing amoebas stood at the sides of the door like sentries on backlit pedestals.

He heard the sound of a door slamming and a shadow danced across the hall—what he could see of the hall from the open bedroom. "Suzette?"

Tony rose and slipped on his trousers, too self conscious to roam a stranger's house naked. Not to mention that Suzette's near perfect form made him feel less than adequate in his own private jumble of bones and flesh.

He approached the hall. A dark figure, illuminated from behind by the bouncing light from the fireplace in the living room, cast an evil shadow on the wall. A shadow with a gun.

The sound of a click! echoed down the corridor.

Kozol ran silently back towards the bed, picked up his shoes and shirt from the chair where Suzette had tossed them in their climbing passion, unlatched the sliding glass door and ran out onto the redwood balcony.

Cold hit him.

It was like diving belly first into ice water.

Tony heard a shot and then another. He hopped over the railing into the darkness below. Pain rattled his feet as he ran headlong down the steep hill to the trees below. Kozol fell several times, bruising and lacerating his body, mostly his bare feet.

He came to a stop and looked up. All he saw was black. "Where the hell did the house go?" Tony cried wildly. He needed to get back...to help Suzette!

He pushed his shoes over his bloody feet and pulled his shirt over his head. Kozol was completely disoriented now. From the bottom of the valley, no lights shone. No houses, no cars, no streetlights...

Tony grabbed his chest. No coat.

"Oh shit," he muttered, realizing the depth of his predicament. Slowly Kozol picked his way through the underbrush, fighting his near-lightless way through thickets, cacti, sharp stones and shifting sands...hoping for some sign of a trail upward...

Wondering what the hell had happened back at the house... The strange woman he had seen had short dark hair. It wasn't Suzette. What had happened to Suzette?

Tony worked his way painstakingly back up the pathless hill. And when he got to the top, there was nothing. The house was gone. But with sick reality sinking in, Kozol realized that the house wasn't lost, he was.

Tony turned in a circle, decided on a direction and began walking. His path took him up and down a low ridge. Kozol stopped when he reached water. Was it Oak Creek, he wondered? Could he follow it to civilization? Or would it lead him into Arizona's fathomless bowels and near-certain death?

Tony sat on the ground and bit his lip. He didn't know. He heard a rustle of leaves from deep within the belly of the forest. A bird...a snake...mountain lion? What had that guide said about poisonous rattlesnakes and big cats? Did they eat people?

A gentle breeze carried Kozol's scent in the direction of the unknown sound. He'd seen enough movies to know that wasn't good.

He didn't know to where and there was no point trying to surmise. It didn't make a bit of difference. He just had to walk.

Or freeze to death...

TONY STOPPED to rest under a looming pine tree. A large outcropping of red rock sheltered him from the breeze that blew across the valley floor. Deathly cold with no jacket and worn out from marching, he sidled up beside the tree and closed his eyes. Tall Arizona sycamores, like giant silvery skeletons rose malevolently against the stark ground. Crucifixion cacti stood like foot soldiers waiting their marching orders.

Kozol eyed this all helplessly. A tiny light flickered on the side of a remote mountain. It could have been someone's home, with electricity and running water, shelter and food. Tony dozed off gazing longingly at the light...

BRILLIANT LIGHT forced its way across the heavens, sending night's creatures scattering for their burrows and their nests. Tony rubbed his eyes and cheeks. The bright sun gave off little heat. This would have discouraged him, but the light gave something blessed in return.

A sign.

A road sign to be precise and a gray road sweeping by towards the east. He'd slept next to a damn road all night!

Tony rose awkwardly and hobbled down the hillside to the road. He walked for what seemed like five miles or more but in reality was probably closer to two. A family of five on their way into town for church services, gave Kozol a ride in an older model yellow sedan. Church. Sunday morning. Tony had only arrived Friday and it seemed like he'd been in Arizona a month.

That's okay, he thought to himself, as the car rolled across the hills effortlessly and his flesh struggled hopelessly against his pain, fatigue and dehydration, for tomorrow was Monday.

And Monday he was going home.

NINE

"MR. KOZOL—" Assistant Manager Mark's face wore a look of astonishment and amusement.

"Tony!"

Kozol turned. The cry, which seemed filled with anguish and relief, came from across the lobby. Suzette, dressed in tight blue jeans and a clinging pale blue sweater leapt into his arms. She squeezed with what must have been all her might because Tony was certain he'd heard something break. Like his ribs. "Hey!"

He set her down. She kissed him. He pulled away.

"Tony," Suzette said, swatting a lock of his hair from his face, "are you okay, baby?"

He nodded. "What about you? What's going on? I heard gunshots! Are you all right?" Kozol rattled off the questions that had been plaguing him all night long in rapid succession.

"Yes, I'm fine." She held his hands as if to calm him. "You disappeared. I've been worried sick about you."

"Disappeared? Somebody was taking shots at me!"

"Shots?" Suzette looked surprised. "I didn't hear any shooting, Tony. One minute I leave you lying in bed and the next thing I know you've jumped off the balcony!"

"But that strange woman—"

"That," interjected Mark, who apparently couldn't resist, "was the owner of the house." He chuckled. "We've heard all about it."

Kozol shot him an ugly eye.

Suzette nodded and took Tony's arm in hers. "That's right. Linda. She came home and heard someone in the guest room, our room, and went to investigate. I didn't even realize she was there. I didn't have a chance to tell her that I had a—" she paused, "guest. The next thing I know I'm hearing shouting and banging— I dropped a glass in the bathroom and shouted myself! Maybe that's what you thought was gunshots? You were confused."

"Scared," suggested Mark.

Tony's eye got uglier.

"Linda thought you were an intruder. She was as scared as you were." Suzette clung to his arm. "By the time I got everything straightened out, you were gone. We looked and looked for you but you had disappeared. I'd never been so scared in my life. I even called the police." She pulled Kozol's arms tighter around her waist.

"You mean I jumped off that balcony for nothing?" Tony was dumbfounded. How could he be so stupid! "I could have wandered around out there for days. I could have died. And for nothing?"

"I know," replied Suzette. "I'm so grateful that you managed. A person could get lost forever out there...but you made it...thank goodness. I don't want to lose you, Tony."

"You won't. I'm a lot tougher than I look." Kozol kissed her.

Mark sniggered.

"I came back to the hotel early this morning to see if you'd returned. But no one had seen you. And it's been so crazy around here this morning, too. What with Annie in the hospital and you missing, why—"

"Annie?"

Suzette nodded. "You know, Miss Campbell. Oh my god, that's right! You haven't heard. It's Annie Campbell who was the driver of the other car."

"Other car?" Kozol found his brain derailed by the sudden turn in the conversation and then it struck him. "You mean the one that was involved in the accident with Virginia?" Tony couldn't believe it.

"That's right. Annie is in the hospital now. Still in a coma." Suzette shook her head sadly.

"But that means that she—"

"Tried to run down Miss Garner," finished Suzette.

"But why?"

"Who knows?" Suzette leaned up and kissed Kozol on the lips. "So," she demanded, pulling Tony away to a quiet corner near the fireplace, "where were you last night? You look awful."

"I feel awful. I spent the night outdoors."

"What!"

"A family found me this morning and gave me a lift back here. Otherwise I'd still be walking around out there somewhere."

"Oh, my poor baby." Suzette gave Tony a tender hug and rubbed his unshaven cheek. "We'll get you cleaned up and get some breakfast, okay? You must be starved."

"Yeah, but first I want to have a word with Virginia. Have you seen her? Does she think Annie Campbell was trying to kill her and, if so, why?"

Suzette replied, "I only wish I knew, Tony. But right now, let's take care of you, okay? I brought your things from the house. They're out in the car."

Tony nodded and allowed Suzette to lead him away.

"Uhum-uhum." Mark Taggert cleared his throat. In his fingers he held up a keycard. "I suppose you'll be needing yet another of these, Mr. Kozol?"

Tony checked his pockets, scowled and snatched the card from Mark's hand. "Thanks," he muttered.

"GET SOME REST," whispered Suzette. Naked, and straddling him on his bed, she ran a warm finger along Kozol's chest. She had helped him to his room, washed him in the shower and led him to bed.

Tony kissed her breasts and pulled her closer. She sighed and pulled away.

"I have a lecture, Tony." She checked the clock on the night table. "In fifteen minutes no less!"

Kozol groaned. "Hurry back."

"I will." She rose and slipped her sweater over her head. Pulled her undies and pants up over her athletic legs. "And you get some sleep."

"I will."

"You want me to have room service send over something to eat? Some eggs and toast maybe?"

Suzette grabbed Tony's hairbrush from the edge of the sink and ran it through her hair.

"Thanks."

"I'll take care of everything." Suzette pulled the covers up over Tony's nude body. "You're driving me crazy like that."

He kissed her. "You're driving me crazy—period."

After she'd gone, he closed his eyes and tried to force himself to sleep. But all he could think of was poor John's untimely death...and Annie Campbell lying in a coma. Had she really tried to run Virginia Garner off the road? Why? It probably had something to do with the crystal skulls.

Kozol tossed his head side to side between the goose feather pillows. He had to help Suzette recover the stolen skulls. He also needed to figure out who killed his friend and why.

Tony dressed quickly, fighting off the soreness of his muscle and bone. One of these days, he told himself confidently, he was going to start an exercise program. One of these days...

Wearing Janvilhelm's leather jacket—not that the pianist was going to need it again—Kozol found his car and drove into Sedona. He checked through the pocket-sized visitor's guide he'd picked up the day before and looked for hospital listings. There was only one big medical center and it wouldn't be hard to find out on Highway 89A.

Along the way, Tony passed the police station. He stopped in and asked for Detective Gibson but was told she was out.

"Who should I say was asking when she comes back?"

Tony gave his name.

"Kozol? Hey, wait a minute. I've got something here on you." He shuffled some papers on his desk. "Here it is. A missing persons report. I take it your not missing any more?"

"No, I guess I should have called earlier and explained."

"Yeah, I guess." The cop tossed the paper to the side and spread his hands across the desktop. "So, what happened to you?"

"I got lost in the dark."

The policeman laughed loudly. "Maybe you should have left a trail of breadcrumbs—"

"I'll remember that next time."

"So, if you didn't come in here to report yourself un-missing, what do you want?"

Kozol explained about helping his friend Suzette and his impending visit to Miss Campbell.

"Yeah, them skulls." The officer grinned. "I heard all about it. But I don't expect we'll ever find them around here. Too high profile for Se-

dona. Whoever took them would never risk showing those things around these parts. Everybody's
into that stuff."

"Are you?"

"Doesn't hurt to keep an open mind. You
never know, do you?"

"You're right. What about my friend's murder? Has there been any progress there?"

The officer, who appeared to be in his mid-
forties, shook his head. "Nope. Sorry about your
friend, but we've got a fuckin' grand piano for
evidence out back. Not exactly a smoking gun—
You know what I mean?"

Tony did. "Any fingerprints?"

The policeman laughed. "Tons of them. You
have any idea how many people have laid their
hands on that thing? The hotel couldn't even tell
us the last time it'd been polished."

"Can I see it?"

"Nope. Captain would have my head, sorry."

"That's okay."

"Now, if you want to see something, check out
that Nissan the Campbell woman was driving—"

"It's here?"

"Yeah, towed out back on the lot. Took a picture of it myself to send to my nephew in Mich-
igan. He's into car wrecks, if you can imagine
that." The police officer shook his head in obvi-

ous wonder, though Kozol couldn't decide if it was regarding the car wreck or his screwed-up nephew. "Amazing the woman survived. Score one for airbags, I suppose."

"Mind if I take a look?"

"You hear me telling you not to?"

"Thanks."

"Sure. If you get lost, just holler and I'll send out a patrol car!"

Kozol avoided making a wisecrack in return. After all, the man was an officer of the law, with a loaded gun on his belt.

Annie Campbell's car sat in the sun beside Virginia's less-battered Wrangler. Annie's car was by far the worse for wear. Tony jumped into the Wrangler. The damn thing still smelled like dog. Inside the glove box he found the vehicle registration. Virginia Garner was from Oakland, California.

The grill of Miss Campbell's car was halfway to the windshield. The doors were jammed shut but the windows were shattered. Tony reached in the stuffed glove box. A flashlight, a tire pressure gauge, tons of receipts, and a service manual. Inside he found the car's registration. Miss Campbell resided in New Mexico. The car had plates to match. No mysteries here.

Tony banged the Nissan's top in frustration. It

was time to pay a visit to the alien-communicating Miss Campbell. He walked the length of the wrecked car. The trunk was still halfway ajar. He lifted the lid and looked inside.

Lying at the bottom of the trunk was an aluminum travel case. Just like the one that Suzette kept Maggie and Azultican in. He pulled the case from the trunk and carefully opened the clasps. The black foam inserts inside were carved exactly in the shapes of the crystal skulls!

He set the aluminum case on the ground and searched the rest of trunk, hoping to find the two skulls in some secreted hiding place. Yet there was nothing but a spare tire and some paper towels.

Kozol wondered why the police hadn't noted the significance of the attaché case. Of course, Suzette had mentioned the missing skulls but hadn't bothered to tell the detective that Maggie and Azul had been in a carrying case. Det. Gibson had only seen the photo of them on the brochure and the misinformation had spread.

Tony decided he would have to straighten the police out later. First he had to have a word with Miss Campbell.

THE SEDONA-OAK CREEK Regional Medical Center sat like a modern day jewel of architecture and medicine on the outskirts of West Sedona. Tony parked in the visitors lot and approached the reception area. He all but expected to see Mark Taggert behind the receptionist's desk.

Instead, the woman facing him looked like Mark's evil twin sister. Except she wore thick black rimmed spectacles. All that was missing was the Groucho Marx nose. Her thick black hair looked like it could stop a bullet.

It stopped Tony.

"May I help you?"

"Yes, hi. I'm looking for Annie Campbell's room. Can you tell me where she is?"

Fingers flicked almost maliciously across a computer keyboard. The receptionist's pinkie slammed down on the enter key as if it were a cockroach. "Room 203, East Wing."

"Thanks." Kozol had only half-turned when the woman stopped him.

"There are no visitors allowed at this time, sir. You'll have to leave."

"Couldn't I have a moment with her?"

"Are you a relative?"

"Yes. I'm— I'm her brother-in-law." He waited for her to call him a liar.

Instead she sighed as if the weight of the world had suddenly been placed on her shoulders and said, "Just a minute. I'll see." Mark's evil twin sister picked up a white phone and paged a Dr. Morris. Apparently he was off. "How about the charge nurse?" A pause. "Okay, thanks, Patty."

"Well?" Tony asked.

The receptionist twisted a stick of gum in her mouth and began chewing. "Hold on. Someone is coming." She pointed to a row of chairs.

Tony sat and studied the tattered magazines, the most current of which had a picture of Jackie Onassis on the cover as woman of the year. That was pretty strange considering the building itself looked considerably newer than the magazine. Theoretically, he supposed, they could have ordered in a batch of outdated magazines for those resigned to wait. Perhaps all doctors' offices ordered from the same place, a depot of timeworn periodicals...

A matronly looking woman in nurse whites arrived and stood over him. She must have been six foot tall and three feet round. Her name tag said she was Debbie Dunn, R.N. "You the relative of A. Campbell?"

Tony nodded. "Yes. How is she? May I speak with her?"

Nurse Dunn shook her head side-to-side. "Funny, when Dr. Morris spoke with Miss Campbell's mother in Santa Fe, she didn't mention a brother-in-law being here."

"I've only just arrived," explained Tony. "Hell of a drive, I must say."

"Yeah." Nurse Dunn turned and began walking. She paused halfway down the East Wing corridor. "Well, come on, young man, follow me."

Tony jumped to his feet and hurried after Debbie Dunn, who, if one believed in reincarnation, as so many at the Crystal Skulls Conference did, was a sumo wrestler in an earlier incarnation. Hell, she could have been one in this lifetime!

They stopped outside room 203. The door was open. Annie Campbell lay in bed.

Still.

Unmoving, but breathing. "She's still comatose," said Nurse Dunn. "But who knows, maybe she'll respond to your charm."

Kozol entered the room quietly, though he wasn't sure if jumping up and down and shouting that the Ramadians had arrived on Earth and had occupied the White House would have woken her. He touched Annie's right hand. There was no response.

Her skin was warm. The only light in the room came from the sun filtering through the semitransparent drapery.

"Annie?" he whispered. "Annie? It's me, Tony Kozol." The room was quiet but for the background noises of exotic machinery whose purposes Tony could only guess at. It was a private room and Miss Campbell's was the only bed.

Tony opened the wardrobe and found Annie's clothes inside. He searched the pockets of her coat but they were empty. And there was no sign of her purse. It was probably locked up somewhere safe.

Kozol returned to the bedside and placed a hand on the comatose woman's shoulder. He gave her a gentle nudge. "Miss Campbell? Annie?" He balled his right hand into a fist. "Damn."

Tony pulled a chair up beside the bed and tried again. "It's me, Tony. Remember me, Annie? Nod if you hear me. Or wiggle a finger. Anything." He watched her body for signs of even the slightest movement.

Nothing.

"I need to know about Magdalena and Azultican, Annie. What was their carrying case doing in your trunk? Why did you have the crystal skulls? Maggie and Azul, Annie, where are they now?"

Hollow, reverberating footsteps passing on the anesthetic looking tile floor outside Miss Campbell's room offered the only sound. The room smelled of disinfectant and urine. "Can you tell me who killed Janvilhelm?"

Kozol felt his heart beating in his chest and

began to count. One...two...three...Tony rose when he reached ten. Another dead end. More wasted time.

"Light."

Kozol gasped and clutched Annie's arm. "Annie?" Her lips had moved. He was certain of it. "Annie, where are the skulls, Maggie and Azul? Why did you try to kill Virginia Garner?"

Annie Campbell's dry lips parted. "Light."

Tony looked around the room in confusion. "You want the light on or off?" He waited for an answer. "Is it too bright? You want me to close the curtains, Annie? Annie?"

"Las Vegas."

"Las Vegas." Tony flopped down in the chair and stared at Miss Campbell. Her lips twitched, then closed. "Las Vegas? Maggie and Azul are in Las Vegas? You stole the skulls to pay for gambling debts in Las Vegas?" Kozol tried desperately to keep Annie talking. "The Ramadians are coming, Annie. They want the skulls. Help them. They're here! Talk to them, Annie!"

Tony shook the woman gently by her shoulders. Annie Campbell's chest rose and fell slowly as a wave licking its way up the edge of the beach. Her breath came out in long, slow pushes.

Nurse Dunn stuck her pumpkin-like head around the door. "Any luck?"

Tony shook his head no. What could he tell her? That Annie Campbell and the Ramadians were planning to take over Las Vegas with the aid of Maggie and Azul, the magic crystal skulls? He didn't think so.

Kozol thanked Nurse Dunn for her time and trouble. He'd have to find the answers elsewhere...

TEN

IF ANNIE CAMPBELL wouldn't talk, then Virginia Garner would. Kozol would see to it. He headed back to the Red Rock Resort—a man on a mission.

Tony passed a small drugstore in a brown, adobe-styled shopping center on his way across West Sedona. He parked the Chevy and popped in to pick up some aspirin. The throbbing, nagging, get-out-of-my-face headache he'd been fighting ever since finding Janvilhelm's body at the piano was driving him crazy.

He surfed the aisles. Aspirin was in the back near the prescription desk. No doubt, the druggists stuck the stuff back there just to make everybody's headaches worse while they searched for it. Another merchandising plot.

Kozol paused, a bottle of generic aspirin in his mitt. He didn't need the woman to turn around to recognize that cute behind. It was the doctor's wife, Camille Kennedy. He took a step back and stood on his tiptoes to watch her over the top of the shelf. She wore tight black jeans. Her long blonde hair cascaded over a brown fur coat that ended at her waist. Real fur or not, Tony couldn't tell.

The pharmacist placed a brown bottle of pills inside a white paper bag which bore the store logo. He stapled a slip to the bag and handed it over to the attractive blonde. She smiled, thanked him and turned away.

Kozol hadn't been able to read what the prescription was for—nymphomania maybe. Tony quickly dropped to the balls of his feet and turned away as Mrs. Kennedy looked in his direction. Hopefully, she hadn't seen him. Slowly he stepped away. He'd wait for her to leave and then go pay himself.

"Tony?"

He froze. Damn. He turned. "Why Mrs. Kennedy," he said with as sincere a sense of surprise as he could muster, "what a surprise!"

Camille held her purse and medicine to her chest. She approached and gave Kozol a friendly hug. "How are you?"

He shrugged. "Okay, I suppose. Needed some aspirin." Tony held the bottle out. Why did he feel so guilty anyway? He had as much right to be shopping at a drugstore as anyone.

"Headache?"

"Yeah, I'm afraid so. It's all this clean mountain air. I'm not used to it."

Camille held the index finger of her right hand up to her lips. The nail polish was pale blue, like her eyes. "You should try a scalp massage—"

"Maybe when I get some free time."

"—And twenty minutes in the jacuzzi will do wonders for you." She snatched the aspirin from his hand. "That stuff will kill you." Camille laid the aspirin back on the shelf, among the cold medicines, and took his hand. "Come on."

"Where are we going?"

"You can give me a ride back to Red Rock."

"Okay, but what about your car?"

She shrugged and led Tony to the front of the store. "Oh, it's not here anyway. Mr. Bernes gave me a lift."

Kozol stopped. "Ralph Bernes?" Big, big Ralph Bernes, who was probably using his psychic powers to find and fry him right now?

"Yes, that's right. He's an old friend."

"So I've heard." Tony looked over his shoulder. "Where is he now?"

"Ralph went next door to the liquor store. I told Owen we'd pick up some extra wine for this evening." Camille started walking again.

"But isn't he going to be wondering what's happened to you? What is he going to do when he comes looking and can't find you?"

Mrs. Kennedy laughed. "I suppose he'll get in

his car and go back to the hotel. After all, he's
still got sessions this afternoon, plus the open
trade show. We're just playing hooky for a
while.''

Tony had the feeling that this type of hooky
was the clothing optional kind. He decided not to
worry about Ralph Bernes. After all, Owen Kennedy was more likely to find and kill him first...

CAMILLE UNWRAPPED her white terry robe and
tossed it carelessly over the nearest chair. A couple of young girls swimming in the large pool
were the only others out. The cold weather had
chased everyone else with any brains indoors.

Tony took a deep breath. Camille Kennedy was
petite but well formed and she filled out her black
and white bikini with ease.

''Come on,'' she beckoned.

Tony dropped his own robe and tentatively allowed his big toe to touch the swirling water. It
was hot. Thank god. Kozol was wearing boxer
shorts, the closest thing he had to a pair of trunks.

He slid down under the bubbling brew, eyes
furtively searching the sidewalks, the curtains and
even the thicker bushes for a sign of either Owen
Kennedy or Ralph Bernes.

''Relax,'' said Camille, as she nestled up beside
him.

Tony wasn't sure which was hotter, the married woman beside him or the water.

She placed one hand on his arm and with the other tilted his head back. "Lean back," she instructed. "Close your eyes."

Kozol allowed her to press his head back against the rounded edge of the outdoor jacuzzi. He closed his eyes. He was good at following directions. Her fingers ran up and down his arm and across his bare chest like a frisky five-footed creature. Mrs. Kennedy reached behind and rubbed his neck stiffly with both her hands.

"How's that?" Camille asked softly.

"Great," he moaned. "So tell me, do you do this for every guy who needs an aspirin?"

Her fingers momentarily paused, then began massaging his neck once more. "It depends…"

"On what?"

"On whether or not I feel connected with that person."

"And you feel connected with me?" Tony wriggled his toes and stretched his legs. His nostrils caught the scent of burning firewood, more aromatic than any incense.

"Yes." She straddled him.

Tony gulped. He didn't dare open his eyes. "Why?"

"There is something special about you, Tony Kozol."

He shifted his legs. Camille went on massaging his neck and arms. "I can't imagine what."

"Maybe you haven't discovered it yet." She ran an errant finger along his cheekbone.

"Got a mirror?"

Camille laughed lightly. "Your outward self is a mirror of the inner self. Allow that inner self to come out—"

Tony cleared his throat and shifted his legs again. If she kept squirming on his lap like that his inner self was bound to come out.

"—and you will become whole."

"I don't know," Tony replied. "I'm just a regular guy trying to get by."

Running a damp hand through his hair, Camille answered, "Janvilhelm saw that something special in you."

"You think so?"

"Of course. That's why he chose you to come here."

Tony gave that some thought. As looney as it was, it was the most sensible thing Camille had said yet. After all, why had John called him up and offered him a music job? They were friends, albeit distant ones as the years went by. Kozol had stayed in Florida. Janvilhelm had bounced all around the world, finally ending up in San Francisco where he had been living when Tony got the call for the job.

But Janvilhelm Rein Wunderkind was successful and could have had his pick of eager, talented musicians. Then again, John was a good guy at heart and Tony was out of work and prospects. A nice guy doing a favor. Everything didn't have to be deep and meaningful. He said so.

"You lack self-esteem, Tony. I can help you with that." Camille led his arms around her smooth, slender waist.

"What about your husband?"

"Owen? What about him?"

Tony was sweating and it wasn't the hot water. "Do you feel a connection with him?" He opened his eyes. He wanted to see her face when she answered.

"A deep one. Owen and I are spiritual mates. We exist as one." A gold medallion dangled between her breasts. A bas-relief of two dolphins jumping through a pyramid.

"And Ralph Bernes? Do you feel a connection with him as well?"

"Ralph is an extremely gifted man."

"I'll bet."

"What does that mean?" She pulled back. The medal lion bounced against her chest.

"I heard you were out here having sex with that Englishman the night Janvilhelm was murdered."

"Who told you that?" she demanded angrily.

"Annie Campbell," Tony said. "She said the two of you were out here in the middle of the night, naked and kissing."

Camille said ominously, "And Annie Campbell is in a hospital bed—in a coma from which she may never recover."

Tony bit his lip. "Meaning what?"

"Meaning that it is bad karma to intrude upon the lives of others. Especially if it has no impact on one's own life. Besides, what was Annie doing out here in the middle of the night? Have you asked yourself that?"

"Yes," answered Kozol. "I even asked Annie, herself. She said she was communicating with the aliens."

"Or maybe she was on her way to get rid of your friend, Janvilhelm."

Tony shrugged. "Why would she want to do that?"

Camille grinned. "You are a naive one, aren't you?" She rubbed his face with the back of her hand. "Janvilhelm had slept with her. Once. At least that's the way I heard it."

"You're kidding?"

"No. After that, he ignored her." Camille twisted a sharp fingernail over Kozol's heart. "She was insulted. Heart-broken. Maybe she wanted her revenge. It is a woman's prerogative, you know."

"No, I didn't." Her nail dug into his skin and he squirmed. "Thanks for telling me. I'll keep it in mind."

"You do that." She leaned forward again, pulling herself closer, their faces almost touching.

Tony felt her warm breath on his face. "Do you think she killed him?"

"Who knows? Maybe."

"What about Maggie and Azul? Who do you think would steal them?"

Camille tilted her head to the side, her golden hair catching a fading glint of sunlight from the west. "Poor Suzette. Without the skulls, I don't know what she'll do. It will be hard for her to continue on the circuit. The crystal skulls were a big draw for her."

She ran a warm finger down the top of his nose.

"You know, Tony," said Camille, "maybe Annie took Magdalena and Azultican. After all, they were crucial to her communication with the Ramadians."

"You may be right there," admitted Tony. He remembered the aluminum carrying case he'd discovered in the trunk of Annie Campbell's car. But where were Maggie and Azul presently?

"Or perhaps dear Ralph—"

"Ralph Bernes? Why would he steal the crystal skulls?" More importantly, why would Camille want to implicate her lover? Tony realized there was more to Camille Kennedy than appearances showed.

"Ralph has always had his eye on the crystal skulls. Didn't you know that it was through Ralph Bernes that Suzette first learned of the skulls' very existence?"

"Is that so?"

"Yes. The way Ralph tells it, he met Suzette at a New Age conference several years ago in Bath. It was there that he was approached by an ex-patriot Mexican living in Sevilla. This man told him about the skulls. And, fool that he is, Ralph told Suzette."

"Then what happened?"

Camille smiled. "Suzette beat him to them. By the time dear Ralph made up his mind to chase the story down, Suzette had been to Mexico and made a deal for the skulls. End of story. My god, but Ralph was furious!"

"I'll bet."

"Of course, when he calmed down he tried to

buy the skulls from Miss Aristotle. He made her many generous offers—more than generous.''

''But she refused to sell?''

''That's right.'' Camille shrugged. A strap of her bikini top fell off her shoulder and she made no attempt to replace it.

''Did Bernes make Suzette another offer recently—here in Sedona?''

''I couldn't say.'' Camille rocked lightly side-to-side in his lap.

''Do you think he's capable of stealing them?''

''Ralph,'' she said without hesitation, ''is a man of great passions.''

''Yeah, I'll bet.''

''Now,'' said Camille, bending forward, her lips half parted, ''as I remember, we came here to help you…''

''Tony!''

Kozol's eyes leapt from Camille's seductive face to the path to the left. The tall man in the dark blue down-jacket and knit cap could only be Owen Kennedy. His grin didn't look so impish this time. In fact, it didn't look anything like a grin at all.

Next to Dr. Kennedy was Ralph Bernes in a long black coat and matching cape. He looked literally explosive.

But that was nothing compared to the third

member of their trio—the one who was screaming and crying even now—Suzette!

Tony jumped. "Dr. Kennedy! Suzette!"

Camille fell back with a splash. "Hey!"

Dr. Kennedy and Ralph Bernes stopped at the edge of the jacuzzi. Suzette remained some paces away.

"Hi, baby," Camille said lightly. "Hand me my robe, please?" Owen carefully picked the white robe off the chair and helped his wife into it. "Thanks," she said, giving her husband a hug. "It's freezing out here." Camille gave Suzette a particularly triumphant looking little smile. Suzette's eyes darkened.

Owen turned to Kozol, whose only hope at that particular moment was that a whirlpool would open up and suck him clear to China. "See you tonight, Mr. Kozol?"

Tony nodded.

"Good afternoon, then." Dr. Kennedy took his wife's arm and strode off. Ralph Bernes followed closely behind. But the look he'd given Kozol before he left could only be described as that of evil delight.

"Damn, how could you, Tony?" Suzette stood alone, sobbing.

Tony rose, painfully aware of his condition, and his thin boxer shorts. "Suzette—" he tried to explain, "it was nothing really. I had a headache and she was giving me a massage. It wasn't even my idea!"

"Oh, please…"

"Really, I only wanted to question her about Janvilhelm's murder! And about Maggie and Azul." Tony struggled against the odds. "I was only trying to help you—"

Suzette wiped her eyes. Her words rained down like a verbal stoning. "I can't believe I fell for you. Men are all alike, aren't they?"

Suzette ran off, out of sight around the side of the poolhouse. She hadn't given him time to answer. But then, he had no answer to give.

The two girls in the swimming pool were giggling and furtively glancing in Kozol's direction. He snatched up his hotel robe and covered himself. Tony put the hood down low over his face. This was a good time to be invisible.

Kozol winced and vigorously rubbed his temples with his fists. Oh good, his headache was back…

ELEVEN

AN EVEN BIGGER headache was waiting for Tony outside his room.

Ralph Bernes.

He was grinning.

Kozol wasn't.

"What do you want?" Tony fumbled in his deep robe pockets for his keycard and stuck it in the door handle.

He was halfway in the room when Bernes answered. Ralph stuck his big paw against the door and said, "That was quite a little scene back there."

"It wasn't what it looked like," retorted Tony angrily. He took out his frustration by tossing the plastic card across the room. It flopped like a one-winged bat and collapsed on the bathroom tile.

"Too bad," said Ralph Bernes. "It looked—shall we say—delicious."

Tony turned, his face mottled. Only this time the red was anger and not embarrassment for a switch. "Shall we say goodbye?!" He pointed at the door which had swung shut behind them.

"Now just a minute, Kozol!" Ralph Bernes

seemed to sweep himself up like a gigantic grizzly bear trying to impress his enemies—or his prey.

Either way, it worked.

"I want a word with you!" he thundered.

Kozol pulled the sash of his robe tightly about his waist. "I'm listening."

"You'll stay away from Camille, if you know what's good for you."

Tony was riled. "Is that a threat, Bernes?"

The big man grinned churlishly. "Let's call it a premonition—a dire premonition. You keep your hands off her."

"Shouldn't this be the good doctor's speech? Besides, there's nothing going on between me and Camille. She did have a few choice words to say about you though, Ralphie-boy."

Bernes glared down at Tony from across the room. Tony had the feeling that Bernes could squash him like a gnat under his thumb if he so chose.

"Such as?"

"Such as," began Kozol, "that you were quite interested in the crystal skulls yourself."

"So what?"

"So, you tried to buy them from Suzette and she wasn't selling. Perhaps a little thievery is your style. You don't seem to be overwhelmed with moral principles from what I can see."

"You're a boor, Kozol. A boor and a fool. Do you think I need Magdalena and Azultican that badly? I am doing quite well as things are now."

"Still, it must have irked you that Suzette got the best of you." He eyed Bernes carefully. "Frankly, you don't look like the type to take losing gracefully, Bernes."

Ralph folded his hands across his big chest. "Life is full of little setbacks, ripples across a still pond. Sooner or later I am certain Miss Aristotle and I could have reached some arrangement. Now—" He shrugged. "Perhaps Miss Campbell will be able to tell us where the skulls are once she is recovered sufficiently."

"She's still in a coma last I heard," Tony replied. He didn't tell Bernes about discovering the skulls' carrying-case in Annie Campbell's car. "You think she took them?"

"She has the most to gain. Miss Campbell has a special—unique—bond with the crystal skulls. But," continued Ralph, "that's immaterial really. Even if she hasn't taken them, she may be able to communicate with Maggie and Azultican, who themselves will reveal their location to us."

"That still leaves Janvilhelm's murder and his murderer is still out there somewhere. Do you think that the crystal skulls can help us with that one?"

Ralph's dark eyes narrowed. "Ah, but I have already helped you with that riddle, Kozol. You simply lack the wit to solve it."

Tony fought back the urge to jump the oversized charlatan. After all, if Ralph Bernes had any answers, Kozol wanted them. "Then how about spelling it out a little clearer for me?"

Bernes merely smiled. "No, I think not," he said, scratching his bushy beard. "Perhaps, someday, a little light bulb will go off in your head." He laughed loudly. "For give me—a small joke."

"Very little."

The psychic put his hand on the doorknob and turned. "I will tell you this, Kozol, if you do find the skulls, I'll pay you handsomely. How does twenty-thousand dollars sound?"

"That's very generous of you."

"And," added Bernes, "I don't care how you get them. No questions asked, as they say."

"That's nice to know. But those skulls could be hundreds or even thousands of miles away by this time."

Bernes tapped his forehead lightly with fingertips. "My intuition tells me that is not the case. Maggie and Azul are near here. I can feel it."

"Well, all I feel is the damn cold. Care to point me in the right direction before you leave?"

"If I knew where the skulls were, I wouldn't

be buying your services now, would I? You could try the Chief, however.''

"Chief Howling Wind?"

Bernes nodded.

"Why him? What's the old chief got to do with the crystal skulls?'' From what Kozol had seen, the old coot was more ceremonial figure-head than anything, rambling on incessantly, his voice a low, unintelligible susurrus at best. Something to dress up the New Age proceedings.

"The good Chief has stolen Maggie and Azul once before, you see. At least, he attempted to—''

"You're joking?"

"Certainly not, Mr. Kozol.'' He released his hand from the doorknob. "It was last year, I believe, at our annual seminar in Orlando. Howling Wind tried to smuggle the two crystal skulls out in his luggage. But he was discovered.''

"Was he prosecuted?"

"No, he apologized most profusely to Miss Aristotle and all was forgiven. As far as I know,'' Bernes added obliquely.

"And why would Chief Howling Wind steal Maggie and Azul?"

"He is part Mayan, you see. Chief Howling Wind feels that the crystal skulls belong to his people.'' Bernes shook his head as if passing judgement. "He's wrong, of course.''

"Of course," scoffed Kozol. "Anything else?"

Bernes paused to consider. "I think not," he said. "I wouldn't want to—overtax your mind."

"Get out!"

Ralph opened the door. He looked back. "We may despise one another, you and I, but business is business. You find the skulls and bring them to me— Twenty thousand dollars, Mr. Kozol."

THE CHIEF WASN'T hard to spot. After all, even in a town like Sedona, you didn't see too many individuals sporting feathered headdresses.

Tony interrupted the elderly Indian as he spoke to two ladies, decked out in matching white and yellow gardenia patterned dresses, in the exhibit room. "Chief Howling Wind?"

The old Indian turned. "Yes?"

"Tony—Tony Kozol." He extended his right hand. Kozol couldn't help noticing that the Indian looked a lot like Willie Nelson, including the ponytail.

"Yes, I remember you, son," said Chief Howling Wind, shaking Kozol's hand warmly. "I have been enjoying your music greatly. The Spirit guides you, I am certain."

"Uh—thank you. Do you think I could have a word with you—" Tony glanced at the two ladies, "—in private?"

Chief Howling Wind nodded and offered his apologies to the women. The two men retired to a corner of the room near the side doors. "What is troubling you, my son?"

Tony took a second to compose his questions. He didn't want to offend Chief Howling Wind needlessly. After all, Tony wasn't even positive that Ralph Bernes had been telling him the truth.

"It's about Magdalena and Azultican."

"The crystal skulls, yes. Such a loss. There is a pall on the entire conference. Who can explain—murder, robbery. The world is full of such good," he swept his withered dark hands through the air. "But it lies beneath the surface. And Evil lurks about. We need to polish our souls, Mr. Kozol. Polish away the Evil and let the Goodness be exposed. It is there," he said solemnly. "It is there."

Tony scratched the back of his head. This was going to be tougher than it looked. "Listen, Chief, I don't mean to offend you, but according to Ralph Bernes you once tried to steal the crystal skulls—"

Chief Howling Wind lowered his head. "Sadly, that is so. I am ashamed."

"You mean you really did try to steal the skulls?"

"Yes. Whatever Mr. Bernes told you, I am sure it was the truth."

Tony hesitated. "I have to ask you this."

"Yes?"

"Did you take Magdalena and Azultican this time?"

"No," answered Chief Howling Wind. "What I did then was wrong. Just as I told Miss Garner—"

"Virginia?"

"That's correct. She asked me about the skulls. It seems she knew I had tried to take them once before. You know, Mr. Kozol," said Chief Howling Wind, "she was trying to enlist my aid in attempting to purloin the crystal skulls herself. She promised to return them to the people of Mexico. As much as I desire this—as much as I believe in my heart that it is the proper place for Magdalena and Azultican—I told her it was wrong."

"What was Miss Garner's reaction?"

"I would like to think that the young woman was enlightened, though who can say? I told her that if she went through with her plans, she would not be able to live with the guilt growing inside her. Do you know what she said?"

"What?"

"Miss Garner laughed and said she already had enough things growing inside her and that one more wouldn't matter."

"How did Virginia know you had taken the skulls once before?"

"It is no secret. Someone told her, I suppose…or perhaps the shadow of regret shows on my face." Tony studied the aged Indian's wrinkled dark skin. His brown irises seemed to be holding back his soul.

"My Spirit was filled with Evil," Chief Howling Wind said. "I let it take control of my Goodness. Though I believe in my heart that the crystal skulls belong to the peoples of Mexico, I was wrong to commit such a selfish crime against another. And the skulls would not permit it."

"What do you mean when you say that the skulls would not permit it?"

"Magdalena and Azultican gave me away, don't you see? I was trying to right a wrong by committing another wrong. The crystal skulls refused to be used this way."

Tony felt like pulling hair, his own or the chief's, it didn't much matter which. "I still don't get it. How did Maggie and Azul prevent you from stealing them away?"

Chief Howling Wind grinned patiently. "The world of the Spirits is new to you."

"Very much so."

"I was in my room, packing," explained Chief Howling Wind. The Indian stared past Tony at the hills beyond, visible through large plate glass windows. "Maggie and Azul were wrapped up in clothing, deep within my suitcase which was on a chair near the bed in my hotel room. I had taken the crystal skulls earlier from their traveling case. Suzette's room was next to mine. It wasn't hard to watch for her to be gone and the maid to be in and out doing her housekeeping, leaving the door wide open…tempting me."

Chief Howling Wind sighed and continued. "I stole into Suzette's room and took the skulls from their case. They felt warm in my hands, liquid with energy and mystery. I waited, sweating with fear I would be caught, making sure the hall was clear, then hurried back to my room. Then I carefully hid Magdalena and Azultican in my own luggage. I rolled them up in clothing and zippered the suitcase shut."

"Then why didn't you get away with it? Guilty conscience?"

The chief grinned. "Miss Aristotle returned with Dr. Kennedy and Rose Blackwood."

"Rose Blackwood?"

"A local Orlando psychic."

"They had come to my room to see me off. The seminar was over. All I had to do was get on a plane and fly away..."

"So what happened?"

"The crystal skulls."

Tony waited.

"They wouldn't let me get away with it, don't you see? We were all standing there talking when my suitcase fell off the chair. Maggie and Azul rolled out on the carpet and stopped near my feet, their eyes looking up at me accusingly."

Tony made no reply.

"I shall never forgive myself. Nor shall I ever forget the shame."

"How did Suzette take it?"

"She was quite upset, of course. But very forgiving." The chief's eyes twinkled. "I've seen you with her. Is the Spirit of Love dancing near?"

"I don't know," Tony answered honestly, as much shaken by the question as by the change of tack. Suzette was special. And crazy.

Of course, there was Nina Lasher, back home in Ocean Palm. She had helped save Kozol's hide when the police had suspected him of murdering that gangster, Michael Razner. Since then, she and Tony had developed a romance of sorts.

Now he was confused.

Suzette overwhelmed him. She was full of wild energy, aliens and magic skulls—whereas Nina was a bookkeeper, feet firmly planted on the ground. Nina made him feel safe. Maybe he should call her?

Then again, he should find Suzette and try again to explain…to apologize.

Tony only hoped Chief Howling Wind was right about the very forgiving part. Kozol hadn't spoken to Suzette since being caught with Camille on his lap in the spa. Tony may have been out of the jacuzzi, but he wasn't out of hot water yet.

"Follow your heart," instructed Chief Howling Wind, as if reading Kozol's thoughts. "It seldom lies."

"I'll do that," answered Kozol, though at this point he had no idea where anything was going, least of all his heart. "Thanks, Chief." Tony had to say one more thing before leaving. "About that suitcase of yours, Chief— Things fall, you know?"

Chief Howling Wind looked at Kozol as if he had heard it all before. "It was very stable, I'm sure."

"Well, even so, zippers break."

The chief shook his head. "No, the zipper wasn't broken."

TWELVE

IT WAS CAT AND MOUSE...or rather mice.

Tony was the cat and Virginia and Suzette were the mice. Neither woman answered their room phones and neither responded to his steady pounding on their respective doors.

Kozol dressed for dinner—in the best of the clothes which Suzette had bought for him. He was going to have to pay her back. When was Owen Kennedy going to pay him for the weekend anyway? He was beginning to worry. Especially after having been caught in that embarrassing situation with the doctor's wife earlier.

What if Dr. Kennedy simply refused to pay him? What recourse would he have? What did he have the nerve to do about it anyway?

Not much.

But two thousand dollars was a hell of a lot of money to lose. Not to mention the thousand Janvilhelm had promised him. That money was no doubt gone. Kozol didn't even know who his friend's family were let alone how to find them.

And with John killed, Tony wasn't about to ask any survivors for money. Of course, if Nina were here, she would insist on it. She would have insisted that he have a signed contract with Owen Kennedy as well before performing. Not for the first time was Kozol made aware of the fact that Nina would have made a better lawyer than he had ever been for all his years of training.

That reminded him, he still owed her a phone call. At least there was one woman who would talk to him. But first, dinner.

This was the Sunday night banquet. Final thoughts and parting hugs. Food aplenty and drinks galore. And, hopefully, paychecks.

Kozol glanced at himself in the full length mirror on the back of the bathroom door. As good as it gets, he mused sourly.

He shoved his room key in his jacket and headed for the main lobby. Tony stopped at the entrance to the banquet room and took a deep breath. Suzette, wearing a liquid gold gown, sat beside Ralph Bernes. Dr. Owen Kennedy was on the other side of Bernes and next to Owen sat his wife Camille. Camille had dressed to the nines as well in a high collared zebra-skin dress, a dress so tight Kozol could see her stomach move slightly with each breath she took.

There were two empty chairs besides Tony's— Janvilhelm's and Annie Campbell's. One dead and the other comatose. Kozol's tented name placard was between Janvilhelm's and Annie's, but he didn't think anyone would mind if he switched places with Janvilhelm. He knew Janvilhelm wouldn't.

Tony sat. Suzette moved her chair away, closer to Ralph Bernes, who couldn't resist grinning. Chief Howling Wind sat across from Tony, dressed incongruously this time in wrinkled blue jeans, with a crisp, long sleeve white shirt over which he was wearing a vest of many colors.

"Good evening, Tony," said Dr. Kennedy politely. He leaned over and offered Kozol a glass of wine. "Cheers."

Tony took a sip. "Cheers." Poison?

Suzette leaned over and whispered something Kozol couldn't catch in Ralph's ear. The Englishman guffawed. Tony bit his lip and ignored them as best he could.

To hell with them all, he decided, taking another sip of the white wine that now half-filled his glass. Tomorrow he would be home. His flight was scheduled for twelve-thirty in the afternoon. All he had to do was make it through the night. Maybe have a leisurely breakfast in town and then it was practically straight downhill all the way to Phoenix.

Back to Florida, warm, sunny Florida. And

Nina Lasher. At least she wouldn't be whispering in some other man's ear.

So caught up in his reverie was he that Kozol didn't even notice that Chief Howling Wind had risen from his seat and taken the empty chair beside him. Annie Campbell's chair.

The old chief laid a heavy hand on Tony's arm. "How are you, my son?"

Kozol shrugged. "Fine, Chief. You?"

Chief Howling Wind lifted Annie Campbell's name card in his fingers and flipped it over and over. "I hear she is stable."

"How do you know that?"

"Owen has been in frequent contact with the hospital. He's quite concerned about her. She is a friend, after all."

Tony nodded. "I went to see Annie myself."

"How was she?"

"Fine. I suppose. Not that she had much to say."

"She spoke?" The chief seemed quite surprised at the news.

"No, not exactly. She—she babbled a bit."

Chief Howling Wind leaned closer, the smell of alcohol and tobacco on his breath. "What did she say exactly?"

Kozol paused. "I don't remember. Nothing, really. I mean, I'm not even sure she was awake.

She mumbled something about the light and—''
Tony stopped. ''That's all.''

''Her injuries are quite severe, I'm told. But she
is strong and of good heart. She will recover.''

''You know, Chief. There's one thing I haven't
told anyone—not even the police.''

''Yes?''

''I was poking around in Annie's car. They've
got it out behind the police station. Anyway, in
the back, in the trunk, I found the case.''

''The case?'' Chief Howling Wind scratched
his cheek with a long, yellowed nail. ''What case,
Tony?''

''That carrying case thing—the one that Maggie and Azul were in,'' explained Tony.

''What!''

Kozol's head snapped as his shoulder was
roughly pulled in the opposite direction. Suzette
was staring at him with a look of surprise and
outrage on her face.

''Where are they?!'' Her agitated voice rose
above the crowd.

''Shhh. Calm down, Suzette,'' Tony beseeched.
''I don't know where the crystal skulls are.''

''But Annie Campbell does,'' said Suzette, her
brow wrinkled in thought. ''And I'll bet she killed
Janvilhelm, too.''

''Annie? I don't know,'' Kozol replied.

Chief Howling Wind added, "Miss Campbell seems hardly the type to let herself become possessed of a violent spirit, Suzette."

"I wouldn't be so sure, Chief. Annie has always been jealous of my relationship with Magdalena and Azultican. I believe she wants to keep communication between the Ramadians and Earth to herself. Stealing the skulls would give her access to all their secret knowledge. Think of the power she'd have!"

This was all getting a little too esoteric and other worldly for Kozol, who preferred more earthly motives. "But we're forgetting about Janvilhelm," he said. "What reason would she have for murdering him? He's got nothing to do with the skulls."

Everyone at the table was listening now. Ralph broke in. "This is all quite tiresome. Dining should be a festive occasion. Maggie and Azul will turn up. After all, the crystal skulls contain powerful forces which cannot be suppressed. I'm certain that Magdalena and Azultican will find their home—their proper home." The big man looked pointedly at Kozol. A subtle reminder of their implicit agreement.

Camille Kennedy grinned and pulled a long strand of blonde hair across her lips. "Consider this," she began with a smile, "the murder of

Janvilhelm was a crime of passion. Janvilhelm loved women…at least—temporarily.''

"Meaning what?'' Bernes demanded.

"Meaning that Annie Campbell was spurned by Janvilhelm—'' There were several audible gasps as Mrs. Kennedy continued with her theory. "So she kills him in a crime of passion. Slams the piano top down on his head.''

Tony suppressed a shudder.

"And the skulls? Why would Miss Campbell take Maggie and Azul?'' Chief Howling Wind posed the question.

"Don't you see?'' There was no response but the shaking of heads. "To escape. She'd committed a murder. Annie didn't know what to do or where to go and she probably needed money. Maggie and Azul are worth a small fortune to the right person—'' She shot a furtive glance across the table at Ralph.

"But she could have left right away and she didn't,'' countered Tony. "What was she waiting for?''

Suzette answered. "Remember, Tony? Annie was found in her car. Maybe she was trying to escape then. After all, you said the carrying case was in her trunk.''

"But Virginia Gardner was there as well,'' added Bernes.

It made sense. "Annie could have been meeting Virginia. Virginia was drunk—and upset—when I saw her in Tlaquepaque. Annie could have arranged to sell Maggie and Azultican to Virginia. She was desperate for them."

Dr. Owen Kennedy, who had until then remained uncharacteristically quiet, suddenly spoke. "So what went wrong?"

"Who knows?" Suzette replied. She lifted her own wine glass and sipped delicately. A sharply dressed waiter began laying plates of food around the table. "Annie Campbell could tell us, of course, if she wasn't lying so helplessly in that hospital bed."

"Cheer up, Suzette. That's one thing we can be grateful for," said Owen. "When I spoke with Dr. Morris earlier he expressed that he was actually rather hopeful for Miss Campbell's recovery."

"Oh, really? How wonderful." Suzette raised her glass. "To Annie."

They toasted.

"You know," said Kozol. "Annie isn't the only one who can shed some light on all this. There's Virginia."

"Ah, yes, the mysterious redhead," Bernes commented.

"Where is she by the way?" Tony asked, eyes

scanning the tables. "Has anyone seen her to-night?"

No one had. Mysterious indeed.

"I saw her earlier," mentioned Chief Howling Wind.

Kozol asked, "When was that?"

The elderly Indian gave it some thought. "Late this afternoon. After I spoke to you, Tony. She was participating in the alternative healing mo-dalities workshop being led by Miss Guild."

"That's right," Dr. Kennedy said. "I remem-ber seeing her there myself. It was a most suc-cessful session. Miss Guild is a certified regres-sionist, Tony. Quite phenomenal."

Bernes laughed. "Certified? Certifiable is more like it! I think that woman's psyche has flown a little too close to the sun one too many orbits!" He laughed again at his own small joke.

"I've received instruction from Miss Guild, myself, Ralph," replied Camille. "She's also an expert numerologist and she helped me im-mensely with my chakra alignment."

"I wouldn't trust her to align the tires on my Fiat," scowled Bernes.

"What's wrong, Bernes," chided Tony, "afraid of a little competition?"

Ralph Bernes rose and pushed back his chair. "I've had enough." He grabbed his big coat off the back of his chair and threw it over his shoulders with a dramatic swirl. "I shall be in the bar." He took two giant steps, then turned. "You know, Mr. Kozol," he began, "it is a shame you are not a pianist."

"Why is that?" Tony couldn't help but wonder.

Ralph beamed, the jet black hairs of his beard rising like the quills on a porcupine. "Because then, Mr. Kozol, perhaps you would be lying crushed inside a grand piano instead of Janvilhelm."

Bernes, forever the gentleman, bowed to the ladies and departed.

"Ignore him," said Suzette.

"I am sorry," added Dr. Kennedy. "We're all upset, what with Janvilhelm's sudden death and Annie in the hospital. Usually we all get along quite well, don't we, darling?" He squeezed his wife's hand.

Camille smiled. "Yes, of course." She folded her napkin. "Speaking of which, I really should go check on Ralph, don't you think?"

Owen agreed. "Of course, Camille."

Camille rose, lightly pecked her husband on the cheek and wound her way through tables.

"Now, I suggest we get down to dinner before

it gets cold," Owen said, taking up his fork, "and to kinder, more elevating thoughts."

Tony rose. "I'm afraid you'll all have to excuse me, too. There's something I need to do." Kozol stood up and ignoring everyone's polite protestations, made his way out of the banquet room. The only thing worse than a cold dinner was a cold trail. And the trail to his friend's murderer was getting colder by the minute.

Tony only had until morning, but he promised himself that he would do everything he could until then to find Janvilhelm's killer.

He turned down the dimly lit corridor that led to the bar. Bernes and Camille Kennedy were in a poorly lit booth in the far corner, sitting across from one another. Camille faced the wall. Ralph looked upset and the doctor's wife seemed to be offering solace. Something Camille was quite skilled in giving.

Bernes looked across the room and locked his black eyes with Kozol's. Feeling foolish and horribly like a peeper, Tony turned heel.

Besides, there were more important things to worry about than Owen Kennedy's roaming wife. That was the good doctor's problem.

Virginia Garner didn't strike Kozol as the sinister type. But there was something she wasn't telling…

THIRTEEN

HE BANGED ON the door of room 330.

There was no answer and the room was still dark. Not even a crack of light escaped from the edges of the closed curtains.

Kozol banged louder…harder. "Open the door, Virginia!" Bang. Bang. "Come on!"

He pressed his ear to the door—a family getting out of a station wagon, mom, dad, a young boy and girl stared at him as if he were a criminal— not a sound.

Angry, Tony scanned the parking lot for several moments before remembering that Virginia's vehicle was in the police impound.

Cursing and hungry, Kozol headed back to Mystic Hall. Maybe he had passed Virginia. There were so many different paths from the rooms to the main building. It was just possible that she had gone to the last night party and he kept missing her. Then again, she could be avoiding him. Hell, if he had to, he'd camp outside her door until she came clean.

Passing through the side door of the lobby, the

lounge entrance—the bar was aptly named the Spirit Lounge—Tony overheard Ralph Bernes' obnoxious snarling.

"Come on, Suzette," Bernes was saying loudly, belligerently, "Stop playing games! You give me what I want and—"

Tony peeked around the corner, ignoring the young waitress's ugly look. Suzette and Ralph Bernes were up against the bar. A wide-screen television silently played above them.

Suzette looked to her left and saw Tony's puzzled expression. "You're drunk, Ralph," she said, pushing the Englishman away. "Why don't you get yourself a nice cup of coffee and sober yourself up."

"What?" Ralph said indignantly.

"You heard her," Kozol said, stepping up to the bar.

Bernes turned, looked silently at Tony who glared unyieldingly, and back to Suzette. He bit his lip and left. The ground fairly shook beneath the big man. Kozol had to wonder how much longer the earth could go on supporting the brute.

"Thanks, Tony," said Suzette. "Poor Ralph is drunk."

"Yeah, you'd think a big guy like that would hold his liquor better."

Suzette agreed. "Imagine him coming on to me like that."

Kozol replied, "Maybe I should have punched him."

"Don't be silly," Suzette answered. "There's no need ever for violence. I can handle myself with any man."

"Sure. Besides," Tony said, examining his own most average of fists, "it probably would have bounced off all that blubber."

She laughed and picked up her purse where it lay on the bar. "Goodnight, Tony."

"Wait—" Kozol reached for her arm. "Suzette, couldn't we talk? I want to explain!"

Her bright blue eyes sparked. "What is there to explain? I know what I saw."

"But you don't know why. Camille was all over me—"

"Thanks for reminding me—"

Tony sighed. "All I was trying to do was get some information!"

"And you don't care how you get it, do you?" Suzette tossed her head back. A solitary tear rolled down her face. Her sweet scented black hair fell in soft cascades.

Kozol wanted to reach out and touch it. He leaned closer.

"No, Tony." The tear hung on her cheek like a battle scar. A battle of emotions.

"Fine," Kozol said. "I give up. I only came back here looking for Virginia, anyway."

"That figures."

"She may know something about the crystal skulls or even Janvilhelm's murder. I looked for her in her room but she wasn't there."

"Oh, really. I'm not surprised."

"Why is that?"

Suzette shrugged and pulled a tissue from her purse. "I believe I saw her wandering about here earlier—with a rather handsome young man, as I recall."

"Did she say anything?"

"I didn't speak with her. Her left arm was bandaged. I saw her go to the front desk. Perhaps she was checking out. Virginia could be long gone by now, Tony."

"I doubt it. But I'll go ask at the desk. If I have to, I'll camp outside her door. I'll break the door down if I have to!"

"Wait." Suzette held onto Kozol's arm. "Maybe you should talk to Virginia later."

"What? Why?"

"Because," said Suzette softly, "maybe we should talk, Tony."

THE STRAWBERRY BLONDE working the desk had a pleasant, elfin face. Tony took that for a good sign.

"Excuse me, miss," he began, placing open hands on the counter. "Could you tell me if Miss Virginia Garner is still registered here?"

The clerk examined him with pale gray eyes. Her fingernails were painted black. Quite a contrast to her ghostly white skin. "No, sorry."

"Oh, I see," Kozol said, with disappointment. "Can you tell me when she left or if she left an address where she could be reached?"

"No, what I mean is that I can't tell you whether or not a particular guest is registered at Red Rock or not. It's against our policy, sir." Her inky fingernails drummed the counter to some elusive rhythm.

"But Miss Garner is a friend of mine."

"Sorry." Her eyes turned away from Tony and studied the small, portable color television tucked next to the computer terminal.

"Here ya' go, Sandra." A slim youth tossed a keycard over the counter. He had a leather tool belt cinched around his waist.

"Everything okay in 121?"

"Yeah, just needed a washer."

"Great."

"Anything else?"

Miss Black Fingernail Polish, otherwise known as Sandra, looked at her Things To Do Pad. "Nope."

"Gonna get some coffee then. You want some?"

Sandra shook her head no. Eyes back to the television.

Tony cleared his throat. "Well—" It was as if he didn't exist. He surreptitiously extended his hand over the counter and down. Sandra ignored him.

Kozol grinned, self-satisfied. The plastic keycard was now in his pocket. And hopefully it was a master.

TONY HESITATED. Technically, he supposed it was breaking and entering. But technically, they had to catch him. The parking lot was quiet, caliginous and deserted.

Kozol looked at his watch. It was nearly midnight. He rapped lightly with his knuckles. There was no sound from within and not a trace of movement. Where the hell was Virginia, anyway?

He looked left, then right. The hotel rooms on either side were quiet, though there was a light on in the room to the left. Kozol pulled the key card from his pocket and slowly slid it into the slot.

Tony paused, his fingers clutching the edge of the card. He took a nervous breath and waited.

The light turned green.

Tony twisted the knob and entered. The room was as black inside as it had looked from the outside. He quickly went inside and just as quickly closed the door shut behind him. The last thing he needed was to be caught sneaking into a guest's room with a stolen key. The place smelled of perfume and, oddly enough, sweat socks.

Kozol whispered, ''Virginia?''

There was no reply. That was good.

Tony fumbled his way over to the front window. There was a small round table there with a lamp, he remembered.

He turned it on.

Virginia lay in the big jacuzzi tub across from the king-sized bed. She was naked and the tub was full. A few tenacious bubbles clung to existence. But not Virginia.

Virginia's head rested on a pillow. Her eyes were closed. Her mouth half-open. Her skin horribly jaundiced.

Kozol had the terrible, sinking feeling that she was dead.

That was not good.

FOURTEEN

THE RED AND BLUE LIGHTS reflecting off Det. Gibson's bloodshot eyes did little to improve her appearance. She wore a tattered gray parka and sweat pants and smelled of cigarette smoke.

The six squad cars in the Red Rock Resort parking lot, with their well-armed drivers, looked ready to defend the Earth from invaders. Then again, in Sedona, that wasn't such a far-fetched idea.

An ambulance crew rushed inside. It was the duo who had been on duty the night that Janvilhelm had been killed—Burly and Burlier—the man with the black moustache, whose name Tony didn't know, and the woman whose name, as he recalled, was Marge.

"What's the big fuckin' idea, Kozol?" Det. Gibson squashed a chewed up cigarette beneath her heel. She turned and gave an ugly look to a small group of guests awakened by the lights and commotion. "Get them the hell out of here!"

Two officers sauntered over to the onlookers and hustled them back.

Gibson stared at the body.

Tony had the feeling she wished it were he. "Like I told the lady on the phone—"

"You used the phone?"

"Yeah."

"In the room?"

"That's right. What was I supposed to do?"

"Oh, good," Det. Gibson scowled. "Now we won't have to worry about finding any fingerprints."

"I didn't want to leave the body—" Kozol stopped. He didn't want to think of Virginia Garner that way. "—Virginia alone."

"If you're right and the lady's dead, I don't think she would have minded."

A uniformed officer had propped open the room's door with a chair.

Tony added, "Besides, what are you worrying about fingerprints for? Like I said when I called 911, Virginia committed suicide."

They were standing over the naked body now. It looked horrible. Virginia's throat looked hideously swollen and her skin jaundiced. A bottle of scotch, three-quarters empty sat on the back ledge along with a lone glass with the Red Rock logo.

There was a green collection of bottles, shampoo, conditioner, massage oil, all Red Rock freebies. A bottle of purple bath salts stood beside them.

An elderly man, with a crescent moon of silvery hair along the back ridge of his head, wearing a windbreaker with the words *Medical Examiner* stenciled on the back, was bending over the body. Burly and Burlier stood silently by, a stretcher between them.

"You see," pointed Tony to a water-stained, rough-edged piece of paper beside the tub, "there's the note."

Det. Gibson leaned forward and read the paper. "I'm sorry. Please forgive me." She sighed. "How quaint. So, a suicide?"

The medical examiner grunted. "Not likely." He wiped his hands on his slacks. "Found a bottle of temazepam in the bathroom and this bottle of scotch here. An autopsy will tell us if she'd actually used them."

"So what's the problem, Leonard?" Det. Gibson demanded, impatiently.

He pointed a skeletal finger at the bottle of bath salts. "I'd be surprised if those bath salts are hotel issue."

"Virginia liked to take bubble baths—" Tony injected. "She told me so herself."

The ME grunted. "Shoot all this," he said, waving to the scene. A young, plain-clothed man with short, kinky black hair, began taking photos.

"You can take the body when he's done. I'm going home."

"What about the autopsy?" asked Det. Gibson. "And what about those bath salts!"

Leonard shrugged his bony shoulders. He looked at Det. Gibson sleepily. "Whenever I can get to it."

Tony was beginning to like the guy. Anybody that could get under Gibson's thick skin won his approval.

The ME turned to the ambulance crew. "Careful with that one. Use gloves." He turned back to the detective. "If I were you, I'd get a sample of that water."

Det. Gibson scowled at the medical examiner's back side and began barking orders. Then she noticed Kozol. "What the hell are you still doing here? You're fucking with the scene of an investigation!"

HE'D MISSED his plane.

Tony rolled out of bed. The carpet was cold beneath his bare feet. It was nearly noon. The phone on the nightstand began screaming and he'd remembered what had woke him in the first place. This time he answered it in time. "Hello?"

"Tony, it's me, Suzette."

Kozol rubbed his unshaven face. "Morning."

"I thought you'd gone."

"No. Didn't you hear what happened?"

"No, what?"

Tony explained about finding Virginia's body in her room.

"My god, that's terrible!" Suzette said sympathetically. "I spent the night at my friend's house. I didn't know. Poor Virginia. Are you alright, baby?"

"Yeah. But that's why I'm still here. I couldn't see leaving with so many—" he almost said *bodies,* "—loose ends."

Suzette said softly, "I'm glad you didn't leave...without giving us a chance to say goodbye. Can you come over?"

Kozol rubbed the crud from the corners of his eyes. "Sure, I suppose so. Give me an hour to get cleaned up. I'm not positive I can find the house though." Memories of his near-death encounter in the desert came to mind. He didn't care to repeat the experience.

"Okay. I'll tell you what. Meet me at the hotel. I have to come and clear out my room anyway. With the conference ended, everybody's packing up and moving on."

Tony nodded. He'd be moving on himself soon. Janvilhelm and Virginia's deaths made him all the more motivated to do something positive with his life. To do the things he cared about. New challenges...

Kozol stopped himself. It must be something they pump into the air here. He laughed inwardly.

"Tony, are you there?"

"Oh, yeah. I'll meet you in about an hour."

"Okay, you know my room number?"

"Yes, I remember."

Tony rung off and hit the shower. It was ratless. Hooray-hooray.

He dressed quickly and flipped on the television while he did so. Hoping for some local news about Virginia Garner's death. There was none.

KOZOL KNOCKED ON Suzette Aristotle's door.

There was no answer. He glanced at his watch. He was early. Tony paced up and down the sidewalk to keep warm. A light breeze was blowing across the courtyard. At the side of the building, he watched as a blue car slowed to a halt by the curb. The passenger was Suzette. He recognized that lustrous black hair from afar.

She hopped out, said something to the driver, who looked vaguely familiar but was too far away to place and started skipping down the hill from the road. Suzette saw Tony, stopped, then ran towards him.

After removing herself from his embrace, she kissed him lightly on the lips. "Let's go inside."

She unlocked her door and Tony followed her in. Suzette kissed him again.

"So," she said, "going to stay forever?"

Tony laughed. "How could I do that? What would I do?"

"Sedona is full of opportunities."

"But you don't live here year round, do you?"

Suzette replied, "More or less. I'm traveling a lot. But I think of this as my home. I have a little house in New Mexico as well."

"New Mexico? That's where Annie Campbell lives, too, isn't it?"

"Why," Suzette replied, "that's right. The poor dear. Have you heard anymore about her condition?"

Tony shook his head no. "That girl that dropped you off—who was she? She looks familiar."

"Her? My roommate. The girl I'm staying with. You remember her." Suzette began picking cosmetics off the bathroom sink and placing them in a small green case. She glanced at the clock.

"Not really. As you'll recall, I was busy jumping off balconies."

"You probably saw her around at the conference."

Tony nodded.

Suzette grinned and grabbed Kozol by the collar. "I'll have to properly introduce you now, won't I?" She looked at the clock again. "I'd better finish packing and check out before I get charged for an extra night. I wouldn't have taken the room at all," she explained from the bath, "except that the house is so far away to be driving back and forth in the middle of the conference."

The phone rang.

"Could you get that for me, baby?"

"Sure." Kozol picked up the receiver. "Hello, Miss Aristotle's residence."

"Get her!" the voice commanded roughly.

"What? Get who?" The voice on the other end was deep and muddy.

"Get Aristotle."

Tony was annoyed. "Who the hell is this?"

"Who is it, baby?" cooed Suzette from the bath.

Tony put his hand over the mouthpiece. "I don't know," he exclaimed. "They won't say."

"Ask them what they want."

Tony demanded, "Who is this and why do you want to speak to Miss Aristotle?"

There was a pause and then the word, "Crystal."

Tony's eyebrows twitched in confusion.

"Cry—" Then he understood. It was the crystal skulls. "Where are they? Have you got them?"

Another pregnant pause and deep breathing. "She pays—she gets them. Now put *her* on the phone! We're not talking to anybody else!"

Kozol fought his anger and gripped the receiver tightly in his fist, squeezing it like a stick of clay.

Suzette stuck her head around the door. "What's going on?"

Tony whispered, "It's Maggie and Azul." Suzette's face went from shock to glee to shock again. "I think whoever this is has them and wants you to pay to get them back." He thrust the telephone at her.

Suzette nodded nervously and put her ear to the receiver. "Yes?" She nodded several more times and said, "I see." Gently, she put the phone back in its cradle.

"Well?" Tony asked.

"You were right. My god, Tony, they've got Magdalena and Azultican!" She leaned against his shoulder and cried.

He held her. "What are you going to do?"

She looked up at him with those strong blue eyes, now aswirl with tears. "I'm going to do just as they ask."

"I'll help you. What do they want?"

Suzette shook her head no. "No, Tony. I have to do this alone—like the kidnappers said."

"But I can help—"

"I'll be alright." She took Tony's hands in hers. They sat on the edge of the bed. "They want ten thousand dollars."

"Ten thousand!" Kozol wasn't going to be much help there. "Dr. Kennedy owes me some money. I can give you that much. It's only two thousand though."

"Thank you, baby, but don't worry," Suzette answered. "The money is not a problem. I can pay them. I will be happy to pay them to get back my children."

"So," said Tony, "when are you meeting them?"

She put a hand to his lips. "No more questions."

"But this could be dangerous! You're talking about meeting criminals. You could be in danger yourself!"

"No, my instincts tell me that all will go well. I believe," Suzette said solemnly.

Tony shook his head in disbelief. "But I could come along just to be sure."

She silenced him again. "Promise me that you will let me handle this myself," she insisted. "I know what I am doing and I want to get my children back. If this is the way that I can, then I must comply. You must, too.'' She took his face in her hands. ''I love that you are willing to risk your own safety to help me, baby, but promise me that you will let me handle this.''

Kozol couldn't resist those eyes. He gave Suzette his word.

FIFTEEN

"HEY, KOZOL!"

Tony peeked over his shoulder. Ah, yes, that delightfully disgusting voice was that of Det. Gibson, Sedona's one-woman creepshow.

"Hey, yourself defective." Kozol turned his attention back to the front desk where dear old Mark was arguing with him about room rates for his unexpectedly extended stay.

"Ninety-five is the very best I can do," Mark said flatly.

"Fine." What choice did he have? Unless Suzette wanted to let him stay up at her friend's house... Maybe he should broach the subject.

"What did you say?" Det. Gibson breathed down Kozol's neck. A not pleasant sensation.

Tony turned. Det. Gibson was fashionably attired in a black suit that an Amish man would have thought dated with comfortable, square-toed, highly polished black shoes.

"I said 'hi, detective'."

Sedona's finest scowled. It was like observing a glaring, albino pumpkin as the lit candle in its skull transmogrified its face from pumpkin to devil. "You mind telling me why you didn't tell the police about that case being in Annie Campbell's trunk?"

"Gee, Det. Gibson, I was certain you would have noticed it."

"Very funny. Of course we noticed it. No one knew it had any relevance, that's all. That dizzy woman with the skulls never bothered to tell us they'd been in a carry case for Christ's sake."

"Have you talked to Annie about it?"

Det. Gibson grinned. "Just about to. Seems she wakes intermittently and her doctor called to say she was awake enough now to question."

"Have fun." Kozol took a step.

"Not so fast, Kozol." She gripped his arm. Tony had no idea flesh could be so damnably cold.

"Now what?"

"Miss Campbell wants to see you, that's what."

"Me? Why?"

Det. Gibson shrugged, pulled an unfiltered cigarette from her front jacket pocket and lit up.

"Excuse me, detective," Mark stated. "But one is not allowed to smoke in the lobby, I'm afraid."

Det. Gibson blew a cloud of smoke in the assistant manager's pudgy face. "One is not allowed to have a bunch of friggin' dead bodies cluttering up their hotel either *is one?*"

Mark held his tongue.

"But you don't see me jumping all over your butt about it, do you?"

Without waiting for a reply, Det. Gibson grabbed Kozol by the shoulder and led him out to her unmarked official car.

"CAN WE GO IN?"

The nurse nodded and stepped aside.

Tony entered the room first. The curtains were drawn shut. The room was silent and smelled of disinfectant. There was a large bouquet of flowers, red, yellow and orange, in a glass vase to Annie's left. "Annie?"

Annie Campbell, head half-buried in her thick pillow, opened her eyes.

"Hi, Annie. It's me, Tony." Her eyes quivered, shut, then opened and seemed to refocus. Tony wondered if she could see anything at all, understand anything at all.

She smiled. "Tony." Her voice cracked. It was almost a whisper.

Detective Gibson pushed Kozol out of the way. "I'd like a word with you, Miss Campbell." She took out her little notebook. "We've identified the case in the trunk of your car as being the carrying case of those two skull things. I'd like to know just where those skulls are now," the detective demanded.

"Detective—"

"Shut up, Kozol. This is a police matter."

"But as you said," Tony replied, "Annie asked to speak with me."

Det. Gibson let out a loud, long and warm breath.

"What was it you wanted to see me about, Annie?" Kozol laid a hand on her bandaged shoulder.

Miss Campbell stared angrily past him towards the detective. "Not until *she* leaves!"

"What?" roared Det. Gibson.

The corner of Tony's mouth went up. He looked at the policewoman.

Det. Gibson leaned directly over Miss Campbell's face and swore. "This is police business." She ticked off points on her fingers. "I've got grand theft...I've got a murder. Probably two murders!"

Miss Campbell weakly raised her right hand. "I'm afraid I'm feeling faint, after all." She winked at Tony and Det. Gibson missed it. "Perhaps I had better get some rest."

"Why, you do look tired, Annie." Kozol did his part. Both looked at Det. Gibson who had her arms tightly locked around her unremarkable chest.

"All right," she said flatly. "But I'll be waiting outside." She turned at the door and said, "But if you're hiding any evidence, it would be best if you cooperate, Miss Campbell. You might get some leniency that way." Det. Gibson stomped off.

Annie grinned. "Quite the playmate you have there."

Tony rolled his eyes. "So, how are you?"

"Better." She folded her hands together atop the bedspread.

"Did you hear about Virginia?" Tony glanced at the card on the flowers. They were from Doctor and Mrs. Owen Kennedy.

"No," Annie sat up taller, "what's happened?"

"She's dead."

Annie gasped. "From the accident?"

"No," explained Kozol, "last night, in her hotel room." Tony explained finding the body and the Sedona Police suspecting foul play.

The clairvoyant shook her head. "That poor, poor girl."

"Poor girl! I didn't expect you to say that after she tried to run you off the road!"

"What?" Annie looked at him for a moment,

not understanding. "Miss Garner didn't run me off the road. I mean, she was swerving a bit as she came around that bend—"

"She'd been drinking pretty heavily. I saw her earlier."

Annie nodded. "That explains it. And then I was hit from behind by that blue car."

"Behind?"

"Yes, and that's the last thing I remember about the entire accident."

Annie's eyes went to the door. Det. Gibson was nowhere in sight. "I was being chased, Tony."

Kozol's eyes grew. "By whom?"

She whispered. "I found Magdalena and Azultican. I'd been out walking, in the desert near the hotel. Trying to cleanse my spirit. I stumbled behind a rock. I saw a glint of light. When I looked to see what it was, I discovered the case with the crystal skulls inside! You can't imagine how surprised I was!"

"What did you do with them?"

"I looked around. I didn't think anyone had seen me. But I knew that whoever took them could be lurking about somewhere, so I slowly, carefully made my way back to the resort and put them in the trunk of my car."

"But why? Why not just give them back to Suzette?"

Annie Campbell sighed. "I didn't want her to have them."

"Annie, the crystal skulls belong to Suzette. You've got to give them back."

"You are right, of course. But once I had them—I couldn't decide what to do with them! So much power!"

"It's not too late."

"But I don't have them anymore, don't you see? I heard all about the police finding out about the case in my trunk. Another officer was here earlier asking the same questions as that detective. I thought for sure I had been caught with them. I was dumbfounded when I found out that the police had not recovered Maggie and Azul." Annie leaned back. She appeared to be growing tired.

Tony didn't know what to say.

"Of course," said Annie, in a wavering voice, "that means she has them…"

"She?"

The astral channeler nodded soberly. "Lindi."

"Lindi?" Hell, she couldn't mean Lindi Light! Memories of he and Janvilhelm's old college friend came flooding back. Lindi and John had been tight. "Lindi who?" he asked slowly.

"Lindi Light." Annie's eyes grew dark. "You know, I had seen her around the hotel the night of Janvilhelm's murder."

"Let me get this straight—" Tony ran his fingers through his hair. That headache was coming back again. "You saw a person named Lindi Light at the Red Rock the night Janvilhelm was killed?"

She nodded. "Lurking. In the shadows. Dressed in dark clothing. But I saw her. I see everything. It was Lindi herself chasing me down the mountain. She hit me from behind and now I am here. In the hospital. Lucky to be alive. She is an evil force—a container with a spirit of evil flowing, circling..."

Kozol was beginning to think that the poor woman was off her rocker. Hell, even under normal circumstances he thought Annie Campbell was off her nut.

"The Ramadians are angry, you know." Annie looked at Tony with all seriousness.

He nodded as if he understood. *As if.*

"How do you know this Lindi Light?"

"She lives in Las Vegas, the same as I."

Tony's mind raced over what he remembered of Annie Campbell. "But you said you were from New Mexico."

She grinned weakly. "Everybody makes that mistake. You say Las Vegas and everybody assumes Nevada. I live in Las Vegas, New Mexico, Tony."

"I'm sorry, I'd never heard of it."

She shrugged. "Few have. But it is a small town. And I've run into Lindi before. She ran a little pet store." Miss Campbell smiled. "I keep parrots. So lovely."

Annie twisted her head and stared into space. "She wants to control the Knowledge." She turned and gave Kozol a chilling look. "We mustn't let her!"

"What does she look like, this Lindi Light?"

Annie thought. "Small, at least no taller than I, with short brown hair, and a little, beak-like nose. Heavyset."

Tony wondered. The Lindi Light he knew could have matched the description, vague as it was, though she'd had shoulder length brown hair and been trim and athletic. But, as Janvilhelm had said so sagely before his death, "things change."

So do people.

"Tell me, Annie, you say you knew Lindi before, in Las Vegas."

Annie said yes. "We used to attend some of the same local events. Not that I was pleased to see her."

"Did she ever mention Janvilhelm?"

"Oh, yes," replied Miss Campbell. "Often. She hated him."

"Did she say why?"

"She might have. I don't recall. We weren't friends. I detested the woman. I believe she harbored great resentment for him, however." Her eyes narrowed. "Of course, that is something that the girl and I can agree upon."

Kozol remembered the rumor he'd heard from Camille Kennedy—that Janvilhelm had once slept with Miss Campbell, then abandoned her. "You know, Janvilhelm and I went to school with a girl named Lindi Light."

"Perhaps they are the same. Was she as venomous and loathsome then?"

"No, hardly. She and John were unofficially engaged. She was even our manager when we—" Tony stopped mid-sentence. Something tickled the back of his memory.

"When you what?"

Tony shook his head. "Nothing. Something somebody said...I don't remember."

Annie patted the mattress. "Sit."

Tony balanced himself on the edge of the hospital bed. It was stiff.

"I've had a vision."

Kozol stifled a yawn. The last thing he needed now was a vision. Unless it was of a tall, cold drink, with Tony with his feet stuck in the sand at the beach, home in Ocean Palm.

"Light plans to use the crystal skulls to take

control of their knowledge. She will try to thwart the Ramadians. Perhaps trick them into giving her their magic. But first she must control Magdalena and Azultican!''

Tony played along. ''And just how is she going to do that, Annie?''

Miss Campbell closed her eyes. Her chest rose and fell. She blinked. ''The beginning of the universe,'' she said, fixing him with a look of All-Knowing certainty. ''She is seeking the power there. The Wheel at the Beginning of the Universe. The energy of this vortex is immense. Lindi is going to try to use this energy to control Maggie and Azul and then the Ramadians themselves! They are in danger! Tony, you must save them!''

Annie half-rose from the bed and Kozol gently pushed her back down. ''Take it easy, Annie,'' he said softly. ''I'll do what I can, I promise. You get some rest.'' Oh, good, now he was promising to save the Earth from aliens! Or was it for aliens?

Hell, he was getting more confused by the hour. Not for the first time, Tony wondered if he was spending too much time in Sedona. All that red rock and mumbo jumbo was beginning to rub off on him.

Annie nodded. ''Tonight,'' she said, ''when the moon has risen over the center of the universe, remember, Tony!''

Kozol solemnly pledged his word. "There's just one more thing, Annie—"

She waited. What else did she have to do?

"If you saw Lindi Light creeping around the hotel Friday night, why didn't you say something to somebody? I mean, why didn't you tell the police the next morning, after Janvilhelm had been found at the piano? You must have been suspicious."

Annie looked like a neatly scolded schoolgirl, but when she spoke Kozol could discern not a trace of remorse. "Yes, I had my suspicions, as you say. But remember what I expressed to you earlier, Tony. Lindi and I shared one thing... And often that is enough, enough to create a bond between two people who would otherwise be enemies." She paused and seemed to stare into space. Maybe looking for the unseen Ramadians for all Kozol knew. "If all she had done was to murder Janvilhelm, then I would not speak. Forgive me, but my hatred for him was at least as great as hers."

"Did you—"

"Sleep with him?"

He nodded his head.

"Yes," she whispered. Annie Campbell folded her delicate hands across her lap. "I am quite too old to be a foolish little girl, am I not?" She grinned wistfully, as if the days of innocence were regrettably lost.

Tony didn't know what to say. Janvilhelm-John had been his friend. Perhaps he couldn't help the way he had treated Annie, for reasons Kozol might never know. "I'm sorry."

She shrugged. "So am I. For everything. Perhaps I should have spoken up. It's simply that, if Lindi had killed Janvilhelm, I found it to be something of a favor. So I kept my silence. As much as I disliked Miss Light, I could see no point in her going to prison for ridding the world of one philandering piano player."

It made sense, in an imperfect way. "Take care, Annie. Rest."

"I will. Come back and see me again," Annie said quietly, "after you've saved the world and our treasured bond with the Ramadians."

Oh good, mused Tony, not too much pressure. Sticking his head round the edge of the door, he caught sight of Det. Gibson pacing like a caged panther, back and forth, up and down, near the lounge. When her back was turned, Kozol lightly plunged down the hall to the right.

If Annie Campbell was right, Lindi had the crystal skulls and that meant Lindi was likely the mystery person who had phoned the hotel demanding ten thousand dollars for the skulls' safe return. That deep, muffled voice on the telephone could as easily have been a woman disguising her voice as a man disguising his.

And Suzette was going to meet her somewhere. She could be in real danger. Of the worst kind!

Furthermore, if the astral channeler wasn't confused or lying about what she had seen Friday night, Lindi may very well have killed Janvilhelm. Suzette could be next!

And that detective would only get in his way.

Kozol made his way down a maze of hospital corridors, coming at last to an employee entrance. He pushed open the door and looked around. A young kid in hospital whites was just getting into his VW. Tony waved and ran towards the car.

"What's up, man?" The young man's thin blonde hair was cut short, military style. He wore tiny, silver earrings in each ear. His hands held the wheel. He had small, sharp teeth.

"I need a ride." Tony pointed vaguely across the parking lot. "My car's broken down."

"Where you headed?"

"I'm meeting a friend at the Red Rock Resort. Do you know where that is?"

The kid nodded. "No problem. Hop in."

SIXTEEN

KOZOL GAVE THE KID a salute of thanks, pulled his key card from his pocket and opened the hotel room door.

All he needed were his car keys. Then he had to track down Suzette.

"Detective!" Tony nearly leapt out of his skin. How the hell had Gibson beat him back to the hotel?

Det. Gibson sat on his bed. Not exactly to Kozol's delight. Her gun was in plain sight on her belt. She gave it a friendly pat. A gesture Tony didn't miss. "Kozol."

Tony shivered. He'd never heard his surname uttered in such ominous tones. "How-how did you get in my room?"

She ignored his question. "What the fuck are you up to, Kozol?" Det. Gibson rose. Though she was shorter than he, she seemed to loom over him. "Fuckin' playing games with me?" She poked him in the chest. "I don't like it."

"As far as I know," said Kozol, summoning up all his reserve, "I am free to do as I please."

Det. Gibson gulped and looked ready to burst.

"You ran out on me back there! I ought to haul your stupid ass off to jail!"

Tony equaled her stare. Her face was blotched a furious red. "On what charge?"

To his surprise, Det. Gibson laughed and said, "You think you're so goddam smart, don't you? Ever hear of Vacor?"

"No."

"It's rat poison. You've heard of rats, haven't you?"

Kozol remained silent.

"The autopsy came up with traces of the stuff in Janvilhelm's body."

He shrugged. "Really, Det. Gibson, I don't have time for all this. I've got things to do."

"Like what?"

"None of your business."

"If it's about those damn crystal balls—"

"Skulls—"

"Balls, skulls—I don't care if they're freakin' crystal chandeliers— If you're holding out on me about them or about these murders, you're obstructing justice!"

Putting her hands on her hips, Gibson seemed to come back to a more even keel. The detective grinned. "And believe me, pretty boy, I'll be happy to charge you."

"Murders?" Tony ignored her threats. "Are

you talking about Garner? Do mean that Virginia really was murdered, too?''

''If not, the lady picked an ugly way to commit suicide. Her alcohol level was through the roof and that bottle of scotch by the tub was laced with that temazepam she had. That's a sleeping pill. She got that in the hospital after cracking up her car—I checked.''

''Sounds like an overdose to me,'' said Kozol, ''and that fits with the suicide note.''

''You ever hear of potassium permanganate?''

''A chemical of some sort, I guess. So what?''

''So your lady friend took a bubble bath in the shit.'' Even Det. Gibson looked upset at the memory of Virginia's naked corpse. ''And it's nasty. According to the coroner, some foolish women have tried to use the stuff to perform abortions on themselves. Trouble is, the amount you need to do the job is often enough to kill the dear mommy as well.'' The detective counted on her fingers. ''There's burning, swelling, shock.''

''Damn.''

Gibson shrugged. ''According to the autopsy report, Miss Garner was probably seriously drunk and soporific when she took that potassium permanganate soak. So she may not have felt a thing.''

''That's something, I suppose.'' Kozol fell

back into a chair. So far, his adventure in the New Age was more deadly than uplifting. "And you're still insisting it was murder not suicide?"

"I haven't told you everything, Kozol. My guess is that the bottle was laced without Miss Garner's knowledge. According to witnesses, the lady had been drinking heavily all evening. She comes back to her room, already half-drunk and, continuing her binge, she starts in on the scotch and decides to take a bubble bath. You said yourself how fond of bubble baths she was."

Tony nodded. It made sense. Horrible sense. Yet who would kill someone in such a gruesome fashion? And why?

"My guess is Miss Garner had some help getting to heaven. But we're getting sidetracked here, Kozol, aren't we? Tell me, what did Annie Campbell say to you back there at the hospital?"

Kozol did some soul searching. How much could he tell this Sedona police woman without jeopardizing Suzette's chances of getting Maggie and Azul back?

He knew how important the crystal skulls were to Suzette. Hell, she called them her children! Tony's plan was to help her recover the skulls and then try to capture Lindi Light or at least follow her to see where she went.

Then, he and Suzette could call the police and

have them arrest the woman. A happy ending for everyone.

Then again, Lindi Light could be even more dangerous than he realized. Did Det. Gibson have any idea who killed Virginia? Could it have been Lindi? And why?

"Tell me this, detective—"

"Kozol—" Det. Gibson glared. "I've had enough of your questions. I want some answers!"

"Just this one thing...do you have any suspects in Virginia's murder? Do you know who killed her?"

Det. Gibson grinned a grin that the Cheshire Cat would have admired. "Oh, yeah, Kozol. I know. That's the punch line."

"I don't get the joke," Tony said sourly.

Det. Gibson smiled and said, "I know, that's what makes it so funny.

"So, who did it? Who killed her?"

"We found a print. We matched to a known felon. Also checked with the Oakland PD. Came up with some interesting information at that end. When we reported her death, they went out to her apartment. Guess what the Oakland guys found?"

Tony shrugged helplessly.

"See, not so smart are you, mister ex-lawyer?"

Kozol didn't like how much the detective seemed to be enjoying herself.

"I'll tell you what they found—Miss Garner's apartment had been broken into. Among the more interesting things they found were a bundle of letters, all marked *'Return to Sender.'* Care to guess who she'd been writing to?"

He hadn't a clue and said so.

"Janvilhelm Rein Wunderkind." She waited for his reaction and he didn't disappoint her. "Care to guess what she was writing?"

"I've no idea."

"Miss Garner was begging your friend the piano player to take her back."

"You mean they knew each other before?" Why hadn't John said so? What was the big secret, anyway?

"That's right. Intimately. And Miss Garner was distraught that the relationship was over. I figure she drove out here to face him down."

"Intimately?" Tony remembered the argument he had witnessed between Janvilhelm and Virginia after the opening ceremonies. Janvilhelm had shrugged it off at the time. He had explained it away as a run-in with an overzealous fan or something, as Kozol recalled. "So maybe she confronted John, got angry and, in a fit of passion, slammed the piano down on his head?"

"Could be..."

"So, you were about to tell me— Who killed Virginia?"

"Nice try, Kozol. But I think I'll keep that one under my hat for a while. I will tell you this, however," she paused and helped herself to a long sip from Tony's bottle of water on the night table. "Whoever murdered Virginia killed two people, whether they intended to or not."

"Meaning Virginia and Janvilhelm."

"Meaning," she said tossing the bottle across the bed where it rolled, hesitated and then fell over the opposite side, "that Miss Virginia Garner was three months pregnant—"

"What?!"

"—with Janvilhelm Rein Wunderkind, pianist of the New Age, Mister Screw'em and Leave'em's baby!" She smiled in apparent glee at Kozol's awestricken puss.

Tony recalled the vague comments Virginia had made in the days before her death, about carrying something around inside her, about someone trying to kill her. Had she known her killer? Had she let him or her in her room?

One thing was certain, Janvilhelm hadn't killed Virginia. He'd already been murdered himself and Virginia seemed the most likely candidate for that possible crime of passion.

Det. Gibson dragged him away from his

thoughts. "Last chance, Kozol. You gonna tell me what Annie Campbell told you?"

"She didn't tell me anything. Just some wild talk about aliens and saving the world." He didn't know if the detective believed him. Yet it was pretty much true.

"Fine." Det. Gibson buttoned her coat. "I don't think that ditzy woman can tell me anything I don't already know, anyway." She finished closing up her jacket and fished her car keys out of her pocket. "You know what it's like trying to interview these lunatics that attend conferences like this?"

Tony figured silence was his best route. After all, Det. Gibson, herself, didn't seem to have her feet very firmly planted on Reality Road either.

"Come on," she said, nearly throwing open the door.

"What? Forget it! I've got things to do." There was no way Tony was going anywhere with the police. He had to find Suzette one way or another and if he couldn't help her, at least warn her.

"You're coming with me as a material witness," insisted Det. Gibson.

"You have no reasonable—"

"Kozol, you want to know who killed Virginia, don't you?"

"Yeah—"

"Well, I'm going to show you."

"All right, I'll come with you. But this better not take long."

"Fine," scowled the detective. She pushed him out the door. "Besides, I want you where I can see you. That way I can be sure you keep out of my way!"

Kozol tripped, caught himself and said, "Stop pushing, dammit. I said I'd come and I'm coming." Besides, this way he could get Det. Gibson off his back in time to help Suzette.

In the car, Det. Gibson fired up the engine and said, "I had a call from dispatch while you were monkeying around and sneaking out of the hospital. Got an address on a suspect."

"Got a name?"

"You tell me, smart guy."

Kozol double checked his seatbelt as Det. Gibson without so much as a "how-do-you-do" very nearly took out a big yellow school bus as she unhesitatingly swung out onto Hwy. 179 and again without so much as a glance for oncoming traffic.

He took a shot. "Lindi Light." The disagreeable detective didn't reply to his question. He figured as much.

What he didn't figure on was what happened next...

SEVENTEEN

"HAND ME THAT," Det. Gibson said gruffly.

She took her right hand off the steering wheel, a move Kozol wished she hadn't made at fifty miles an hour. The car veered into the next lane, earning a double-honk from the car beside them. The detective fired back with a triple expletive and Tony quickly handed her the map book.

She held it against the steering wheel and studied it with one eye, while the other was, hopefully, on the moment by moment increasingly dangerous road.

"You need some help with that?" Tony offered.

"Nah, I got it."

Det. Gibson had driven across West Sedona, past the police station and the city hall complex. They headed further out of town now. "There's our road," the detective said, "on the right."

Tony braced himself for the turn. The light had turned softer now, the red less brilliant. Sun going down and the moon would be rising. He wondered how he could keep his promise to Annie Campbell.

Pavement turned to hard-packed dirt. The terrain looked vaguely familiar. Then again, Red Rock country looked all the same to him still and probably always would.

Det. Gibson was whistling as she slowed the sedan and took a steep incline. The road turned into a driveway and Tony's eyebrows shot up.

"Hey!" he said. "I know this place!"

The detective was grinning. "I know. It's the house you fell out of the other night—the night you got yourself lost."

"That's right," replied Tony. "It could have happened to anyone."

Det. Gibson eased the car to a stop in the drive, within site of the double oak front doors.

"How did you know? And what are we doing here?" Chills went up his spine as he remembered his night in the high desert. This house was not exactly a place he felt a keen desire to revisit, despite his more pleasant moments in Suzette's bedroom here. Not to mention, Tony felt like an idiot for having jumped off the balcony in the first place and for no good reason. Not that he was about to admit that to Det. Gibson.

"Just keep quiet and stay in the car, Kozol." Det. Gibson popped open the driver's side door and placed her feet on the gravel. "I'll go ring the bell."

"I'm not staying here!" Tony threw open his own door and slammed it shut behind him. The sound echoed around them like a sharp blast.

Det. Gibson looked furious. "Get back in the car, Kozol!"

"No." Tony crossed his arms. "Not until you tell me what the hell is going on! You dragged me out here. So start explaining. This is Suzette's house. Are you trying to tell me that she—"

Both heads turned as the sound of the front door opening drew their attention. A small, heavyset woman with dark hair stood in the doorway. She was dressed in baggy jeans and a dark parka.

Tony realized it was the same woman who had inadvertently entered his room at the Red Rock Resort his first day there.

Det. Gibson stepped forward.

"This is private property!" shouted the woman. "Turn around. Now!"

That was when Tony noticed the rifle she had cocked in her arms. He was beginning to regret having slammed the door shut and only hoped it would open again as quickly. This looked like a good time to leave and he said so. "Come on, Det. Gibson, let's go."

"I'm afraid I can't do that, Miss Light. I've a

warrant for your arrest." She patted her coat
pocket. "For the murder of Virginia Garner."

Tony stared. "That's Lindi?" The college girl
had changed. Immensely. More than either he or
John. And he hadn't recognized her. "But what's
Lindi Light doing here at this house?"

"She shares it with her sister," Det. Gibson
said under her breath. Louder, she said, "Come
on, Miss Light, put down the rifle and come with
me. It's over now."

"But Suzette said she stayed here with a
friend—" interjected Tony.

"Look, Kozol, this house is titled to Suzette
and Lindi Light."

"Suzette's last name is Aristotle, not Light."

The detective sighed. "I told you her real name
wasn't Aristotle. I mean, hell, who has a name
like that?"

"They're sisters?"

Det. Gibson nodded.

"And Lindi killed Virginia?"

"The way I see it they were in on this together.
Found a print on the bath salts belonging to Lindi.
Lindi here has a criminal record. Checked with
New Mexico. Found a similar print in Oakland."
Det. Gibson turned to Lindi. "You made a little
trip to California, didn't you, Miss Light? Found
a letter of Miss Garner's. Tore off an appropriate

passage, hoping we'd think Miss Garner had killed herself, despondent over Janvilhelm's abandoning her—worse yet, leaving her when she was carrying his baby—"

Tony was shocked. "What?!" Kozol raced round the front of the car and confronted the detective. "You never mentioned finding prints. Why didn't you tell me about this?"

"Like you told me about Annie Campbell or any of the other shit you were up to?" Det. Gibson replied. They glared at one another and neither noticed as Lindi raised and aimed her rifle.

Det. Gibson went down with the first shot. She screamed and fell behind her car door. Tony scrambled beside her, ignoring the sharp rocks cutting his fingers, the red mud ruining his clothes.

Another bullet buried itself in the dirt in front of them.

"Are you okay?"

The detective bit her lip and nodded. Sweat poured from her face despite the cold. She was holding her right arm. "It feels like the triceps." Det. Gibson, keeping low, reached into the car and lifted the radio's mike, giving the operator a Mayday and their location.

Tony pulled back Det. Gibson's torn coat over

her protests. "Why the hell didn't you have some backup if you knew that Lindi was the killer?"

"Figured I could handle it myself."

"Terrific." Another shot. This time into the door. Lindi was playing with them now. "Lindi? Lindi, it's me, Tony. Tony Kozol!" There was no reply. "Come on, Lindi. You don't want to kill me. We're friends!" Kozol raised his hand. His friend took a shot at it.

"Get out of here, Tony!"

He wished he could.

Det. Gibson asked, "Have you ever fired a weapon?"

"A weapon?"

"Yeah, you know, bang-bang—"

"No." And Kozol didn't think this was the place to begin.

"Hear those footsteps?"

Tony pricked his ears. It was the sound of steps scrunching over rock. He nodded.

"She's coming closer…she'll be here soon. Take my gun." Det. Gibson drew aside her coat using her good hand, her left. In the holster was a black gun. What sort, Tony had no idea.

But he took it.

She pointed at the safety and told him how to disengage it. "Now," she said, "take a deep breath, point and shoot."

"Where do I aim?" Kozol held the gun in his trembling hands and prepared to shoot over the top of the door.

"Shit, I don't care. Just hit something!" She winced in pain. "But remember, if you miss—"

Kozol wished she hadn't said that. He slowly started to rise.

The detective pushed him roughly down with her left arm. "You idiot! She'll blow your fuckin' head off!" She whispered, "I'll make some noise— You go round the back and surprise her from the other side."

Tony slid back, crawling as silently as possible, the gun gripped tightly in his hand. Gibson was yelling at Lindi now to surrender. Kozol barely heard the words. After all, his heart was beating ten times more loudly than any vocals. He swivelled around the rear of the police car.

Lindi stood near the center of the hood, rifle aiming down at Det. Gibson.

"No, Lindi, don't!"

She turned in Tony's direction and her finger twitched.

Kozol fired at the same time. Whether he meant to or not, he wasn't certain. Lindi slumped to ground with an anguished cry.

Tony dropped his own weapon and ran forward. Det. Gibson reached the fallen woman first.

"Lindi!" cried Tony. He lifted her head.

The garage door opened and a blue sedan burst forward, burning rubber out of the garage, swerving around Gibson's car and careening down the hill and out of sight.

Suzette was at the wheel.

"Hey, Tony." Lindi grinned weakly. "Long time no see."

"Why did you do all this? Why kill Virginia and what about John?"

"The bastard wouldn't give me my money." She clutched her stomach. Blood seeped between her fingers.

"What money?"

"The money he owed me, the asshole. Don't you remember, Tony? You wrote the contract. John was supposed to pay me twenty-percent of all his earnings."

Now Kozol knew what had been bothering him. Suzette had asked him about contracts when he'd first met her. He had written a contract for Lindi, as John's manager, to collect twenty-percent of his earnings—for life.

"At first it didn't matter much," she explained. "But as he started making so much money, I wondered, why the hell should he be getting rich and me getting poorer?"

Tony said, "But the two of you had broken up, according to Janvilhelm."

"Yeah, he left me—and then he fired me! I end up getting nowhere. Working lousy jobs. Practically living off my sister." She giggled. "That's when I decided to become the rat's number one fan."

"I don't understand—"

"What do you give a rat?"

Tony waited for the punchline.

"Rat poison."

"You gave him the Vacor?"

"Put it in those bottles of scotch I sent him anonymously. Not enough to kill him. I just wanted to hurt him...like he hurt me. The cheapskate didn't care what he drank as long as it was free."

Lindi's voice caught in her throat. "Then I confronted John at the hotel the other night. He was surprised to see me. I showed him our contract. The bastard just laughed and said it wasn't worth shit."

She looked at Tony. "He said you were a lousy attorney and an ex-attorney at that and that his high-priced lawyers would eat that contract up."

Kozol cringed.

Lindi confessed. "So, I dropped the contract

down in the piano. I knew that fool would go for it."

"And then you dropped the piano lid on his head," added Det. Gibson.

"That's right. And pocketed the contract again. And dead's as good as alive. I mean, alive the scumbag would always earn more, but you gotta figure he'd keep squabbling with me over my fair share. Suzette and I reckoned we'd fight the estate for my money. John had no living close relatives so it didn't figure anybody would put up much of a fight over a lousy twenty percent..."

"But why kill Miss Garner?" questioned the detective.

"Don't you see, detective?" said Tony. "Even if Janvilhelm refused to marry Virginia, she was still carrying his baby."

"So?"

"So that baby was John's sole heir." Tony was suddenly struck by the nastiness of Lindi's crime.

"Sounds like Miss Light here wanted to get rid of any competition for Janvilhelm's money. Good thing you weren't in his will, Kozol."

Had it been Suzette's crime, too? Probably. "Did Suzette do all this with you?"

"No, I did it all on my own," Lindi said resolutely. "All the killing."

"You did shoot at me when I spent the night

here, didn't you?'' Tony heard Det. Gibson on the radio again wondering where the help was.

Her eyes twinkled. ''Suzette made me stop. She said she was having too much fun.'' Lindi shrugged. ''But by then you were already gone.''

A helicopter fluttered overhead scattering dirt in their eyes. A squad car wasn't far behind. Tony shouted over the noise. ''What about the skulls, Lindi?''

''What about them?''

''They never were stolen, were they?''

She seemed to reflect, then said, ''What the hell. It was just a little distraction. My sister was only trying to confuse things, cover my trail.''

''Like hell,'' muttered Det. Gibson.

Kozol recalled the anonymous phone call, a call he had taken in Suzette's room. The two women had set him up. Suzette knew he was going to answer the phone—she had asked him to get it— and, when he did, Lindi had gone into her demand-for-ransom bit.

Tony remembered something else that had bothered him in thinking back on the morning after John's body had been discovered and Suzette came in screaming that Maggie and Azul had been taken—

It was Suzette's sneakers. She said she had been out jogging, but her shoes had been spotless.

Kozol's shoes seemed to get filthy with the om-
nipresent red dirt if he so much as walked across
dry pavement. The dirt was practically magnetic!
If Suzette had been out running, her shoes would
have shown some sign of it.

The helicopter landed. An officer and an emergency services technician disembarked. Det. Gibson was shouting instructions. The technician
reached for Gibson's torn arm but she pushed him
off and told him to take care of Lindi Light first.

Lindi was given a shot, of painkiller, Kozol
supposed. "What about Annie Campbell?"

"Her?" Lindi hissed as bandages were draped
round her waist. "I knew she'd seen me after I
slammed the lid on John. I'd have killed her given
the chance. But the next day, imagine my surprise
when she told no one! So I left her alone...until
she stumbled over Magdalena and Azultican. I'd
been keeping an eye on the skulls. I spied Annie
putting the case in her trunk. She must have come
across them in the desert where I'd secreted them
until I could get them back to the house."

"So you decided to get rid of her?"

Lindi grinned wickedly. "I like to think of it
as playing bumper cars for adults. And I couldn't
let her get away with my sister's skulls."

Tony realized sadly that something had twisted
inside Lindi Light. She had seemed carefree and

determined at the University of Miami. What had happened?

A stretcher was rolled out and Lindi strapped down. "See ya', Tony."

From the look of her wound and the drained complexion of her face, Tony wondered if he would...and he couldn't help feeling to blame.

Det. Gibson leaned over the injured girl. "Where's your sister now, Lindi?"

Another grin. It was a lot of grinning for someone who'd taken a bullet. Kozol considered her all the more crazy for it.

"She's gone back to the beginning." A grunt of pain passed Lindi's lips. "Suzette said she was going to make everything right again—"

"What the—"

The man attending to the stretcher stopped Gibson. "She's out of it now, detective."

"Well that's just dandy," cursed Det. Gibson. "Your girlfriend is an accomplice to murder and she could be anywhere by now."

Tony winced at the word *girlfriend.* Suzette had been using him from the beginning.

Det. Gibson finally, grudgingly, allowed the emergency technician to inspect her own condition. "Only a flesh wound," he pronounced. "But you'd better get it looked at straight away, detective."

Gibson promised she would.

"You guys see a blue sedan on your way up?" the detective called to the two officers who'd driven out in the squad car. They said they hadn't. "Well call in an APB and take this guy back to town." She jerked a thumb in Kozol's direction.

Tony said, "I wouldn't do that if I were you, detective."

"And why not?"

"Because I know where we'll find Suzette."

EIGHTEEN

"SO TELL ME wise guy and let me do my job."

She popped one of the pain pills the guy with the stretcher had given her. The helicopter rose noisily in the air and flew out of sight.

"That's just it, detective. I can't tell you."

She looked ready to shoot. Kozol figured it was a good thing her right arm was out of commission.

"But you just told me—"

"I told you I knew where to find her. What I can't tell you is how to get there."

Tony explained. "As you have so painfully reminded me, I don't know the roads and landmarks all that well...not well enough to draw you a map anyhow."

"Go on."

"But I can show you. I can lead you there— If you're up to it?" He looked meaningfully at her wounded arm.

"I'm up to it, Kozol," she said defensively. "But if you're wrong and waste my valuable time..."

Tony cut her off. "I'm not wrong. It's something Annie Campbell told me back at the hospital."

Det. Gibson groaned. "And just what might that be?"

"Annie said that Lindi would try to use the crystal skulls to control the Ramadians and their link with the earth through Maggie and Azul—"

"Kozol—" warned the detective.

"Hear me out, detective! I know it sounds crazy but the other day I took a tour of Red Rock and vortices and medicine wheels and the beginning of the universe and that's where I think Suzette has gone now. It fits with what Annie told me about the wheel at the beginning of the universe."

The detective groaned.

Tony left out the part about saving the aliens. "And it fits with what Lindi herself said about Suzette saying that she was going back to the beginning to make everything right again!"

Det. Gibson rubbed her sore arm. "So you're telling me that Suzette Aristotle—that is, Light, has gone to some medicine wheel, one of those thingamajigs made out of rocks by these nuts who believe in all this mumbo-jumbo metaphysical crap—"

"They truly believe these are places of magical

power of sorts. And I believe that's where Suzette is going."

"To do what? To go time traveling back to the past and make everything right again for her sister? To make right two murders? To get in touch with aliens?"

The irate detective had asked more than one question, yet Tony had only one answer. "Yes."

"Jeezusfriggingoddammumbobumbosonofa—" She hurled open her car door with her left arm and glared at Kozol. "Well, get in for chrissakes!"

They flew down the hill and out onto open pavement once again. Tony gave directions as best he could. After all, he'd only been to the medicine wheel the one time and Brian, their guide, had been driving. But he thought he remembered the way. "Here!" he shouted suddenly, recognizing the turn-off point.

Det. Gibson spun the wheel with her one good arm and Tony prayed they wouldn't hit the embankment. "Now what?"

"Keep going straight for a ways," Kozol said. He watched the narrow road carefully. Somewhere up ahead there had to be another turn-off. Onto a smaller road that would lead them up the big mountain.

"By the way," said Det. Gibson grudgingly,

while her head bounced off the roof of the car, as she blatantly ignored a three foot wide and nine inch deep pothole, "nice shooting back there."

"To tell you the truth," Kozol admitted, "I didn't even mean to fire. It just sort of happened. I was scared. I mean, Lindi was going to shoot—and your gun just sort of went off."

"Nice to know our lives were in such capable hands," wisecracked the detective.

Several miles up, things began to look more familiar again. There was a derelict building to the left which Tony was sure he'd seen before. "Slow down," he told Det. Gibson. "Now, there—take that little road to the right."

Det. Gibson groused. "It's pretty steep here and wet ground isn't going to help." The car slid back and forth while fighting its way up the mountain. Even Brian's Jeep had had a job of it and the ground was even wetter now. Worse still, darkness had all but won the day. The tires spun madly as the mud provided little traction.

"It's Suzette's car!" Tony said. The blue sedan up ahead sat sideways, half-off the road.

"She must have gotten stuck. We're lucky we haven't done the same." Slowly they cruised past. "I don't see your girlfriend."

"She must have gone on by foot. But this proves I'm right."

Det. Gibson nodded and steadied the car. Slowly they continued forward.

But not for long.

Det. Gibson stepped out of the relative warmth and safety of her car and into six-inch deep mud. "That's as far as we're going."

Kozol studied the scenery. "I don't think it's much further. We follow this trail."

A hundred yards along the trail, Det. Gibson stopped. "You smell something?"

Tony sniffed the acutely thin, cold air. "Smoke. That means Suzette's at the medicine wheel. Come on!" He ran forward, ignoring the condition of his poorly conditioned lungs and the detective followed. The moon was their only light now.

The trail ended abruptly. Suzette Aristotle stood near the entrance to the medicine wheel. The wheel itself looked eerily alive. Tony could've sworn it was spinning. With the beginning of the universe in the background—as if beckoning. Smoke billowed languidly from a small stone before her.

Suzette was speaking. Tony saw her lips moving, but couldn't make out the words. She was too far away.

Maggie and Azul sat on the cold earth beside her, glowing with red light that itself seemed alive. Was it the Ramadians? Kozol couldn't help but wonder...

Det. Gibson coughed loudly and Suzette looked up. She'd seen them! Suzette scooped the crystal skulls up in her arms and took off into the trees.

"Damn!" cursed the detective. "Come on!"

Tony nodded. "I'll go this way!" he said, heading off to the left while the detective had taken the right.

He heard Suzette thrashing about in the thick vegetation. "Suzette! It's me, Tony! Stop!"

"Go away, Tony!" she cried in the darkness. "You can't stop me now! No one can! I-I must finish."

The sound of her running had drifted to the right and he realized then that she was heading back to the medicine wheel— To finish whatever it was she had started.

Ignoring the immediate chase, Kozol plunged through the dense bushes in what he figured was the direction of the medicine wheel. He burst through the trees just as Suzette came out a few feet to the left of him.

She screamed and ran for the center of the wheel.

"Stop!" Tony lurched forward, his foot twisted in a root of some sort.

Suzette raced forward, as if fighting Time itself.

She stumbled over the outer edge of the medicine wheel, and half-fell, half-ran to the center. Maggie and Azul had slipped from her grasp and seemed to float in the air like photoluminescent balloons.

As Suzette tumbled into the center ring of the medicine wheel, the crystal skulls came down—Azul on her head. Magdalena by her side.

Tony's breath caught in his throat. Suzette's crumpled figure lay still. Only the crystal skulls seemed alive...

It was then he noticed Det. Gibson standing at the opposite side of the clearing.

NINETEEN

"ABOUT WHAT HAPPENED back there—" began Tony.

He and Det. Gibson were alone in her office now. Kozol was surprised how human it looked. There was a calendar featuring shots of Hawaii on the wall beside her desk, fixed to a corkboard dotted with photos and a bunch of drawings that could only have been made by a child.

And there was a photograph on her desk of what Tony suspected was a husband and a young son, a boy who looked all of seven or eight. There was another photo of the boy hugging the neck of a big white Siberian Husky.

Det. Gibson put down her ballpoint pen. "Back where?" She was taking a final statement from Kozol and then he was free to return home.

"You know, back there—at the medicine wheel… what do you think happened?"

The detective glowered. "I *know* what happened. Suzette Aristotle fell down, struck her head and died. It happens all the time. The mountains are dangerous, especially after dark. You should know that better than anyone, Kozol."

He nodded and played with a paperclip on her desktop. "All the same, detective, did you see the way those skulls—"

"No, I didn't." She turned a sheaf of papers in Kozol's direction. "Read it over and sign it."

It was a copy of his statement. Tony signed without reading. What was the point? Everybody seriously involved was dead. Like her sister, Lindi had died of her wounds. Leaving Tony with a scar that he feared he would face for life.

"You're out of here." Det. Gibson rose.

"Thanks." Tony pulled a dog-eared business card from his equally tattered brown leather wallet. He'd scratched out attorney and written in musician. Now, below that he'd added the word *investigator*. Kozol handed the detective his card. "If you ever need any help with any of your other cases—"

Det. Gibson glanced at the card and her face exploded in color. In retrospect, it had looked to Tony much like the brilliantly energetic red that the crystal skulls had exhibited that fateful night on the mountain at the beginning of the universe.

"Get the hell out of my office, Kozol!"

A GRAVE COFFIN

A COMMANDER JOHN COFFIN MYSTERY

GWENDOLINE BUTLER

Next to the body of the murdered police officer was a note with the scrawled words "Ask Coffin." But what is it that John Coffin, commander of London's Second City police, is supposed to know?

The victim, Harry Seton, was investigating a ring of counterfeit pharmaceuticals, and was also secretly looking into some internal police corruption. Did his cryptic message refer to either case? Or could it be a link to Coffin's other serious concern at the moment: the disappearance of four schoolboys, one of whom has been found murdered?

"...absorbing...classic." —*Publishers Weekly*

Available August 2001 at your favorite retail outlet.

 W(O)RLDWIDE LIBRARY®

WGB392

Kathleen Anne Barrett

Milwaukee
Summers
Can Be
DEADLY

A BETH HARTLEY MYSTERY

**Ex-attorney turned legal researcher
Beth Hartley knows that history often
repeats itself—especially when it comes to
untimely death. The murder of a prominent
CPA sends a buzz through the historical city
of Milwaukee, and the desperate pleas of a
sixteen-year-old boy, the son of the dead man,
draw Beth into the case.**

**Beth's talent for finding the missing links leads
her to a solution as tragic as it is shocking, and
reveals why this Milwaukee summer could
turn out to be quite deadly for her.**

"...you'll be at the edge of your seat..."
—*Rendezvous*

Available August 2001 at your favorite retail outlet.

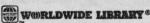

MYSTERY WORLDWIDE LIBRARY® TM

WKAB393

Camille Minichino

A GLORIA LAMERINO MYSTERY

When a janitor from a Massachusetts physics laboratory involved in lithium research is garroted on a dark street—hours after he agreed to accept a huge payoff for overhearing something he shouldn't have—Homicide turns to their prime consultant: feisty Gloria Lamerino, a former physicist from Berkeley.

With her natural ability to snoop and befriend, Gloria skillfully maneuvers her way through the upper and lower ranks of the facility and uncovers a hornet's nest of technical, political and environmental problems just dying to be covered up.

"You'll love Gloria Lamerino and her friends."
—Janet Evanovich, author of *Hot Six*

Available August 2001 at your favorite retail outlet.

The Lithium Murder

WORLDWIDE LIBRARY®

WCM394

Elizabeth Gunn

FIVE CARD STUD

A JAKE HINES MYSTERY

It's a frigid winter in Minnesota, but detective Jake Hines has bigger problems than keeping warm. The body of a man, nearly naked and frozen solid, is discovered on a highway overpass.

As Hines probes the last days of the victim's life, a grim picture of betrayal, greed and fear emerges. But for Jake, solving a murder is a lot like playing cards—figure out who's bluffing and who's got the perfect hand, especially when one of the players is a killer.

"This series gets better and better. Gunn keeps her readers absorbed in the exciting case throughout..."
—*Booklist*

Available July 2001 at your favorite retail outlet.

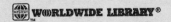

WORLDWIDE LIBRARY®

WEG389

Enjoy the mystery and suspense of

POISON APPLES

NANCY MEANS WRIGHT

A VERMONT MYSTERY

"Wright's most gripping and satisfying mystery to date."
—*Female Detective*

"…Wright doesn't put a foot wrong in this well-wrought mystery."
—*Boston Globe*

After tragedy shatters Moira and Stan Earthrowl's lives, running an apple orchard in Vermont gives them a chance to heal. Yet their newfound idyll is short-lived as "accidents" begin to plague the massive orchard: tractor brakes fail, apples are poisoned.

Desperate, Moira turns to neighbor Ruth Willmarth for help. Ruth's investigation reveals a list of possible saboteurs, including a fanatical religious cult and a savvy land developer who, ironically, is Ruth's ex-husband. But deadly warnings make it clear that even Ruth is not immune to the encroaching danger….

If great tales are your motive,
make Worldwide Mystery your partner in crime.
Available September 2001 at your favorite retail outlet.

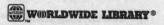

WNMW395

HEAR MY CRY
E. L. LARKIN

A DEMARY JONES MYSTERY

Demary Jones specializes in genealogy and historical research, not murder. But when a sniper opens fire in her office, killing a client, she's very determined to track down a killer.

Soon there's a string of connected murders that put Demary's investigative skills to the test. As she cleverly uncovers both a drug trafficking network and some shocking facts about the people closest to her, she also comes face-to-face with a conspiracy of killers desperate to make Demary's life story a closed book.

"The climax delivers a double dose of excitement."
—*Gothic Journal*

*Available July 2001
at your favorite retail outlet.*

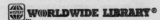

WORLDWIDE LIBRARY®

WEL391